MW01145438

Chapter 1
Why Is Mama Smiling So Much?

"Pack your bags and get out of my house!" Mama screamed as she drew back the belt and hit me across the back once again. Crying I jumped up from the floor and ran to the kitchen to find a paper bag. Where was I going to go? I was only twelve years old. What kind of Mama would put a twelve year old out of the house and for what reason? I had done nothing wrong. My eight year old brother, Lamar, had lied on me as usual, but Mama never listened to my explanations. I ran to the room that I shared with Lamar and started throwing clothes into the brown bag that I had found in the kitchen cabinet. It was better to just do what Mama said than to wait and see what would happen next.

"I'm sick and tired of you! I work hard trying to keep a roof over y'alls head and the least you could do, Gina, is keep this house clean! Just get out!" Mama yelled as she came into the room behind me. At thirty, my Mama, Bertha Jones was a heavy set woman who smoked and drank too much. She wasn't unattractive, but the alcohol and fast life had taken their toll. She looked more like she was fifty than thirty. Her almond-colored skin no longer held its youthful firmness and the worry and frown lines creased her forehead. She had me when she was sixteen and Lamar was born four years later. As a single parent she struggled to keep food on the table and a roof over our heads. She kept looking for the right man that would come along and help her financial situation, but no such luck.

I looked up and saw my brother sitting down the hallway laughing behind Mama's back. Lamar was tall for his age and we were almost the same height, except I had him by two inches at five foot five. He was Mama's complexion having that same almond-colored skin. Mama kept his hair cut short, almost bald, and he was a good-looking kid, except right now I didn't see anything but ugliness as he sat there laughing at me. I didn't understand him. Why did he lie on me and then laugh as Mama beat me and called me names? He was such a mean, sneaky little boy. Always doing stuff, but most of the time Mama would just let him slide. She always said that he was too young to know any better. She took up for him for almost everything, but I rarely got such chances.

Tears streamed down my face as I kept putting clothes in the bag. Finally, Mama ran out of insults to hurl and walked away. I heard the front door slam and knew she had gone outside to smoke a cigarette and calm down. I looked out of the bedroom window and saw that it was almost dark and I had no idea what I was going to do if Mama was for real this time. I stopped packing clothes and laid the bag in the closet and sat down beside it. Why didn't Mama love me like she loved Lamar? I wished I was prettier, maybe then she would treat me differently. I wished I knew my daddy and he wanted me. I could go and live with him. God, sometimes I wished I was never born. Why couldn't I just die and go to heaven? Nobody would ever love or want me? My thoughts were interrupted as my brother sneaked into the room.

"Hahaha, Mama got you good," he laughed as I sat crying in the closet.

"Leave me alone, Lamar." I whispered angrily as I looked up at him. I wanted to slap that smirk off of his face. "Why do you always try to get me in trouble? I have never done anything to hurt you. You know you were lying."

"Yeah, so what? You shoulda let me play with that game yesterday, then I wouldn't a told mama you just watched TV all day."

"That ain't true. Just go away and leave me alone."

"I ain't going nowhere. This my room too. You better shut up 'fore I go tell Mama something else. Uh oh, here she come."

"Gina! Get in here!" Mama yelled from the living room. I ran to where she was and found her sitting on the sofa, watching TV and drinking a beer. I knew what was coming next, a sorry apology and Mama bursting in tears.

"Come here baby. Mama sorry. You ain't gotta go nowhere. I just want you to learn to do what I say while I'm working. It's hard taking care of y'all." Mama burst into tears and pulled me into her arms. "Mama ain't got nobody but y'all. Ain't got no help. One day you'll know what I'm talking about."

I put my arms around her and held her while she cried telling her everything was going to be alright. The smell of cigarette smoke and beer made me nauseous. I apologized even though I knew I had done nothing wrong. No matter how badly she treated me, I still wished she could be happy.

Several weeks had passed since my last whipping and Thanksgiving was only a few days away. Mama had been so happy for the last two weeks. I wondered what was going on. Whatever it was, I was glad because Mama wasn't cussing and yelling at us as much. Even Lamar was acting like a real brother for a change, but that was probably because Mama had just bought him a racing set. He always seemed to get little gifts whenever she had a little extra money which wasn't too often.

"Gina and Lamar, y'all come in here. I got sumptin to tell ya."

Lamar and me ran into the kitchen where she was fixing supper. "What is it Mama?" we asked together.

"Mama got a new friend. Y'all gonna meet him on Thursday. He coming over for dinner. He's a good man. Got a good job. I want y'all to be nice."

"Ok Mama," said Lamar and he left and went to watch TV.

"Gina, you hear me gal? I don't want none of yo' mess."

"Yes ma'am Mama." I said as I followed Lamar to the living room.

That explains why she'd been so happy, a man. I should have known. She acted that way every time. I wonder what this one was like. The last one was married and only came over at night when Mama thought me and Lamar was sleeping, but we weren't. I knew him too and knew his wife and kids. I wondered how Mama could do that to that lady. They grew up together and had been best friends in school.

Any other kid would be happy for the Thanksgiving break. Three days with no school. But at this moment I didn't feel any joy. I regretted being at home with Lamar and on top of that, I didn't want to meet this new man on Thursday. I hated the way she acted around her boyfriends, like some lost puppy longing for its mother. I guess one good thing about no school was that I got to sleep in late because Mama got up early to go to work. She was a waitress at the Waffle Shack. I guess that was as close as our little town could get to a Waffle House. It was located on the main highway that ran through our town and truckers and travelers stopped there for breakfast. I didn't like it. It was always cloudy with cigarette smoke. I choked whenever Mama would take me and Lamar there. I didn't like the food either. Thursday came too fast.

"Gina! Get up and start cleaning up this house. You ain't gonna sleep all day. I got to go to the store 'fore it close and get the rest of the food I need to fix for dinner this ev'nin. And don't wake up your brother. He can sleep until I get back."

I jumped up and almost fell out of the bed. Mama never came in and woke me up quietly. She always had to yell. I looked at my Timex that my grandma had bought me last Christmas. It was seven thirty in the morning. There went my idea about being able to sleep in late. I thought Mama had to work at least a half a day, but I guess I heard wrong. Mama hardly ever let me sleep late when she was home. Not even on the weekends. Lamar got to sleep though. That boy slept hard too. A marching band couldn't wake him up.

"I'm up Mama. I thought you had to work until noon today?"

"Well, Miss Smarty Pants, you thought wrong. I decided to call in sick today so I could get everythang ready for dinner tonight. Now stay out my business and get your behind out of that bed and clean this house while I go to the store."

"Yes ma'am. You want me to mop too?"

"I want you to clean everythang. Dust and mop. You bet' not take all day doing it either."

"Yes ma'am Mama."

By the time I got dressed, Mama had left for the store. This was one of those times I thanked God we were poor. The apartment was small, two bedrooms, a living room, one bathroom and the kitchen. I started cleaning the living room and dusted the furniture. I liked the way the wood shined after spraying and wiping it with the lemon furniture polish. It was some no name brand. We hardly every could afford name brand items, not even in clothes. Although we didn't have much, Mama did have taste and she was a clean woman. The burgundy sofa was against the wall leading to the front door. In front of it was the coffee table. The chairs sat on the right side of the sofa in front of the windows and two lamp tables were on each side. On the wall opposite the sofa was a long stereo set. On the weekends Mama would play her records while we cleaned. Although most people owned CDs, Mama had saved all her old records and had found an antique stereo set at a yard sale. I loved listening to the old music like the O'Jays, Dianna Ross and the Supremes, and so many others. I found comfort listening to music.

By the time Mama got back I had finished cleaning everything but the bathroom. Lamar was still in the bed. Mama brought the groceries in the kitchen and started her cooking. After I finished the bathroom I went to watch TV. I decided to watch my favorite cartoons before Lamar got up. He never wanted to watch what I watched and made a big fuss. Of course, Mama always let him watch whatever he wanted no matter if I was there first.

"Gina, get off your behind and come in here and help me fix this food. I ain't gonna do it all myself."

I quickly got into the kitchen and started cutting up the celery, onions and green peppers for the dressing. Sometimes I felt more like the hired help instead of the child, but I never got any pay or appreciation for it.

"After you finish that, you can slice that cheese for the macaroni. Then, grease them cake pans and put flour in 'em."

I don't know why I had to help fix dinner. I wasn't the one who had company coming over. It was her responsibility. Times like these I wished I was living somewhere else. My only escape was through daydreaming. Sometimes I imagined that she was not my real Mama and my real Mom was out there somewhere looking for me. One day she would show up on our doorstep and tell Bertha that she had come to take me home with her. She would take me to live in a big, beautiful house that had three floors and a lot of different rooms. I would have my own bedroom and bathroom. There would be other brothers and sisters there who would be eagerly waiting for me to come. They would be nice and friendly and treat me like a princess. My real daddy would be there too. As soon as I walked in that big house he would scoop me up in his arms and tell me how much he loved me and missed me. My daddy would tell me how pretty I was and call me his little girl. Snap out it Gina, I said to myself. I had really gotten caught up with my daydreaming that time. I almost dropped all of the cheese on the floor. Good thing Mama wasn't watching me this time or I would have probably gotten slapped for being careless. I guess every kid has a way of escaping reality if only for a little while.

Chapter 2
Thanksgiving Dinner

It was drawing near time for Mama's friend to come over for dinner. Mama was so bubbly and bustling around like a spring chicken as my Grandma would say. I found it all to be quite nauseating. She had been drinking too which made it even worse. Whenever she drank, Mama became another person. Sometimes she would be all sweet and loving, but that lasted about five seconds before the bomb exploded. The best thing to do when she drank was to stay clear of her. The worst one of all was the crying act. She'd just sit and feel sorry for herself. Then, I would have to play the role of the comforter. It was just too much for me. I would never understand what caused her to act the way she did. I swore to myself that I would never be anything like her. There were times when I hated her so much I couldn't see straight and then there were times that I felt sorry for her.

A knock at the door interrupted my thoughts as I was sitting in front of the TV. Mama burst through the living room like a speed of light, showing nothing but teeth. She opened the door and I tried to keep my face expressionless as this old man walked in. Oh Lord! Mama done lost her mind for sure. That man could have been her daddy and my granddaddy. He wasn't gray-haired, but you could look at his face and tell he was real old. He was shorter than Mama too. Now that was funny, because Mama was a tall, plump woman and this man was short and thin. What an odd couple I thought to myself as Mama led him into the living room. I got a really good look at him as he stood in the living room and the light was shining on him. He was wearing khaki pants and a blue gingham shirt. Country! I thought to myself. He had on a pair of black loafers. He even dressed like an old man. As he stood right beside Mama I could see that there was only a difference of a couple of inches in their height.

"Gina, mind yo' manners girl and come over here. Lamar get in here, I want y'all to meet somebody."

Lamar came hurrying down the hallway trying not to look upset at the interruption of whatever he was doing. I stood up and took a couple of steps closer to where Mama was standing.

"Lamar, Gina, this is my friend, Carl Jenkins. Carl, baby, them my two kids I was telling you about, Gina and Lamar." Mama was smiling like she had won a prize or something.

"Hey Mr. Jenkins," I managed to say without cracking a smile.

"Hey," Lamar mumbled as he shifted uncomfortably from one foot to the other.

"Hey kids, nice to meet y'all. You can just call me Mr. Carl." He grinned showing a gold rimmed tooth in the front.

I knew right off that I wasn't going to like him. I thought it was gross that Mama would want somebody old enough to be her daddy. Not to mention the fact that he had brought over his own bottle of liquor. Great, now there would be two drunks in the house. There would be nothing but happy times ahead for sure I thought sarcastically.

"Come on in the kitchen Carl. I got the food on the table. Gina, you and your brother go wash your hands and come on."

I was going to do my best to eat dinner real fast so I could be excused to go to my room. When Mama had company we could forget about watching TV or staying in the living room. That was strictly off limits. They would go in there after the dinner, drink some more liquor and talk about whatever.

Dinner was good as usual. One good thing that I could say about my Mama, she was a good cook. Mama had really laid it out this time. I think all of her food stamps must have gone into buying food for this day. She had made a honey-glazed ham, turkey with all the trimmings, cornbread dressing, collards, macaroni and cheese, broccoli casserole, and her delicious homemade yeast rolls. For dessert, she had baked a sweet potato pie, a pecan pie, and my favorite, a red velvet cake. Everything was good. As we sat there and ate, Mama and Mr. Carl talked. I learned that he didn't have a real job. Not that I was surprised one bit. I could have sworn that Mama said this one had a good job. I should know better by now than to trust anything that she says about her boyfriends. She always saw them through her rose-colored glasses. Mama had a knack for picking men that were low on the totem pole. I guess she didn't see herself as being much. Mr. Carl worked odd jobs and mostly did yard work and painting for the upper class white people in our town. He lived a couple of blocks from us in a house his parents had owned. It turned out that Mr. Carl had a daughter and two sons that were older than Mama. The truth is Mr. Carl had a lot of children and none of them had the same Mama. I learned that while he was sitting there talking about himself. Mama sat there blushing like a school girl. By the time we were finished with dinner, Mama and Mr. Carl had drunk about half a bottle of Seagram's Gin mixed with coke. They were laughing and being silly. It was all getting to be a bit too much for me.

Lamar asked, "Mama, can I go to my room? I'm done eating."

"Yeah baby. Scrape that plate out and put it in the sink, then you can go."

Thinking I could make my getaway too, I asked, "Can I go too Mama?"

"Gina, you ain't doing nothing yet until you clear off the rest of these plates from this table and wash them dishes. Then you can go back there with your brother."

"Bertha, you got a lazy one there I see." Mr. Carl said looking at me showing that silly gold tooth.

"Yeah, she is as lazy as they come. One day some man gonna beat her brains out 'cause she won't keep her house clean." Mama said before she burst out laughing.

Mr. Carl started laughing too. "Here gal, take my plate and scrape it out and your Mama's too."

Tears welled up in my eyes, but I quickly got a grip. I shouldn't have to clean up behind her and her company. One day, I was going to leave this house and never look back. I quickly got the dishes off the table, scraped them out, and ran the dishwater. Mama and Mr. Carl got up and went into the living room. I washed those dishes as fast as I could so I could go to my room and not listen to silly talk and laughing.

Lamar and I sat in the room playing for an hour or so before Mama yelled back there for us to get ready for bed. Good thing we had taken a bath before dinner. All we had to do was change into some night clothes and crawl into bed. Lamar went to sleep as soon as his head touched the pillow. When that boy was sleeping you couldn't wake him up with a bullhorn. I never understood how he could sleep so hard. I lay there letting my imagination take me to places where there was love and happiness. I don't know how long I lay there, but it must have been awhile. I heard Mama tip into our room to see if we were sleeping then she left out. Our apartment was so small, so I could hear whatever was said in the living room. She told Mr. Carl that we were asleep. I guess he was leaving now. Next thing I heard was Mama's bedroom door closing. That was a familiar sound. She always closed her bedroom door whenever her company would spend the night. I waited awhile then sneaked across the hallway to her door. I heard her and Mr. Carl whispering, and then Mama started giggling. I knew that she was letting that man spend the night. To be sure I was going to wake up early in the morning to see if he would sneak out like all the others did. Early the next morning, he sneaked out of the room and left before daybreak just like I knew he would. I was so angry at Mama. Again, I swore to myself that I would not be like her.

Chapter 3
Mama Has Changed for the Worst

It has been almost a month now and Mama and Mr. Carl have been seeing each other almost everyday. Every Saturday Mama goes over to his house and visit for a couple of hours. I am so happy that Lamar and me are old enough to stay at home while she goes. A few more days and it will be Christmas. This is the first Christmas that the three of us will have together. Before Mama got the apartment, we lived with my grandparents. Grandma and Mama got into a big fight and Mama got really mad and said she was leaving for real this time. I thought she would change her mind like before, but a month later we were packing and moved to our own place. I really miss my grandparents because Mama wasn't as mean to me around them.

A week before Christmas which was a Saturday, Mama decided to take us with her to Mr. Carl's house. Although I was curious about where he lived and what his house looked like, I would rather have stayed home.

"Gina and Lamar, y'all get yo' shoes on and come on. We going over to Carl's. And I don't won't no mess out of either one of you or else it's gonna be too bad when we get back home."

We quickly got ourselves ready and went to sit on the porch until Mama came out. I was glad Mr. Carl only lived a couple of blocks because Mama didn't have a car yet. It was a nice Saturday afternoon for December. Kind of warm, but still cool enough for winter clothing, so I could wear my favorite gray sweatshirt with pink teddy bear on the front and my blue jeans. Lamar had on a dark blue warm up suit.

Mama was dressed in a green V-necked sweater and blue jeans. She had taken the time to curl her hair. Mama had thick hair and mine was just like hers, thick and very kinky until a hot comb was pulled through it. My hair was almost to my shoulders and Mama's was a few inches shorter. Mama finally came out of the house, locked the door, and started walking down the sidewalk. We quietly followed her.

Miss Mae, our neighbor, was sitting on her porch rocking as we walked by. She waved at us and smiled. Sometimes Mama would go over there to talk to her and we would play in the yard. Miss Mae's husband, Mr. Lee had died the year before we moved. Miss Mae was a plump old woman in her mid-70s. She had long gray hair and wore bifocals. She had two children, a son and daughter, who came to visit with their families ever so often. I knew the daughter's kids. Actually, I had a crush on the oldest son, Tony. He was a red bone as we would say. He was real cute and quiet. He had two sisters and two younger brothers. His older sister Nikki wasn't very nice and always had something mean to say about me when she was around her friends. Of course, she was unattractive and overweight, but I guess that's how she made herself feel better by picking on other people like me. A few minutes later we turned onto the street that Mr. Carl lived on. As we got nearer to the house I saw that there were a lot of cars parked outside along the roadside.

His house was white and had a huge front porch that wrapped around to the side of the house. It was surrounded by a white, wooden, fence and standing in the corner watching us were two ugly, mean looking black dogs. I don't know what kind they were and I knew this wasn't a good idea because I certainly did not like dogs. Mama interrupted my thoughts.

"Now, Gina and Lamar, y'all better go in here acting like you got some common sense. Don't touch nothing and you better open your mouths and speak if somebody say sump'n to you. Ya hear me?"

"Yes ma'am," we replied in unison.

Mama opened the gate to let us inside and the little dogs started barking, but did not try to come towards us. As we walked up the little sidewalk, I looked at the house. It was an old house, but well-kept. It had wood siding and was painted white with black trim on the windows. The front porch was painted black and on it were three big white rocking chairs. The yard was freshly cut and the hedges trimmed neatly. Since Mr. Carl did yard work, it would have been a shock to me if his yard had been in a mess.

Mama walked up onto the porch and went in through the front door as if she lived there. We quietly followed her. Just as I stepped onto the porch the smell of cigarettes and alcohol almost made me choke. My eyes started watering and I could feel my throat tighten. I suffered with bronchitis and my air passages did not like cigarette smoke, no matter how many times I was exposed to it. As we entered what I assumed was the living room I could hear loud voices coming from the back of the house.

"Carl! You in there!" Mama called out as she kept walking in the direction of the voices.

Mr. Carl appeared in the doorway of the kitchen. Smiling as he watched Mama walk towards him.

"Hey, baby. You show does look good in them blue jeans Bertha. Come on in here and sit down. You know everybody."

Mama giggled and blushed like a silly school girl the same way she did when Mr. Carl came over for Thanksgiving. Deliver me Jesus, I said to myself. If this is the way being around a man makes a woman act, then I didn't want to be a part of it when I grew up. I just couldn't see myself looking so silly and goofy because a man complimented me.

We followed Mama into the kitchen and watched as she sat at a table with about six men that were all strangers to me. There were two more ladies sitting there as well and I assumed they must have been the girlfriends. One of the ladies I knew because she was the sister of Mama's last boyfriend, Bernard.

"Gina, speak up. Don't you hear somebody talkin' to you? Mama snapped.

"Uh ma'am?" I had gotten caught up in my daydreaming again and did not know that Mr. Carl was speaking to me.

"Ginia, I asked if you and your brother wanted something to drink." Mr. Carl said again.

My first thought was to tell him to get my name right, but I knew better. "No sir. Thank you." I could see that Lamar really wanted something and I thought to myself that if he's thirsty then he was big enough to speak for himself.

"Gina, you and Lamar can go outside and play or sit on the front porch until I am ready to go." Mama said as she opened a can of beer.

"Yes ma'am. C'mon Lamar."

We headed for the front porch. As I sat there I looked at all the cars and now understood why so many people were over here. It turned out that Mr. Carl loved to gamble and he would often host gambling parties. He also was a small time drug dealer, but it wasn't one of those deals where he would get rich. He sold a little weed here and there to make ends meet. I heard that through the window as two women, obviously drunk, called themselves whispering in the living room as Lamar and I sat on the porch. Lord! Mama really had hooked up with a "nobody" this time. I don't ever remember her being involved with somebody who did anything illegal. She definitely had lost her mind this time. Didn't she understand how dangerous it was being associated with Mr. Carl? I didn't want to think about it and prayed that God would protect Lamar and me from this foolishness. Lamar and I found ways to occupy time either by playing games or napping in the big white rocking chairs. About four hours later Mama was ready to go and we walked the short distance back to the house.

It was dark and the street lights had come on. Although Mr. Carl's neighborhood wasn't bad, it was still a spooky walk back home because Mama took a "shortcut" that was a little path that had been made through a small strip of woods in front of Mr. Carl's house. It connected from his street to the next street over and our apartment was just around the corner after that. Mama was in the front and of course I ended up in the back. The path wasn't big enough for all of us to walk beside each other. I couldn't believe Mama didn't just stay on the main road that had lights, but who was I to suggest to her that this path might be dangerous at night. Besides she was high on whatever and I did not feel like being slapped down tonight. We made it through the woods okay and got home safely.

"Gina get in the tub and take your bath, then go to bed. Lamar, as soon as she gets out you next. Y'all need to be in the bed. You need to practice going to bed early, next week gonna be Christmas and Santa Claus will be here."

"Yes ma'am." I replied excitedly and so did Lamar. As I ran water in the tub I smiled to myself. Who did Mama think she was fooling? Santa Claus wasn't real. Besides, I had already found the hiding spot of some of our presents for this Christmas. Matter of fact, every year I would find most of our presents. I pulled off my clothes and dropped them down on the floor beside the tub and stepped into the water. The water was nice and hot, just the way that I liked it. I sat down in the tub of bubbles made by the dish detergent. Dish detergent was as close to a bubble bath as it got for this project kid. I don't think we ever used bubble bath. Dish detergent was our universal bubble bath and hair shampoo. Ummmm, the water sure felt good I thought to myself as I slid down underneath the bubbles.

As I sat down feeling the warmth of the water engulf my body, my mind wandered back to Christmas. I was kind of excited. One more week and it would be Christmas. I was getting two new outfits, a watch, and some shoes. Lamar was going to get a new bike, a new jogging outfit, and new shoes. Those were the only things I could find before Mama almost caught me. One thing I could say about Mama and it was that no matter how tough things were with money, she always made sure we had something for Christmas. Mmmm. I slid down farther into the water and watched the steam rise up from its surface. I laid back and closed my eyes enjoying the silence of the bathroom. I'm not sure how much time passed, but when I opened my eyes, most of the bubbles had disappeared indicating that I would soon have to get out and turn the bathroom over to Lamar. Bath time was another favorite of mine. Usually, Mama would leave me alone while I was in the tub and Lamar was no problem because that boy hated bathing and avoided the bathroom as much as he physically could.

"Gina! Get out! Now! Didn't I say take a quick bath?!" Mama yelled as she pounded on the bathroom door.

"Yes ma'am. I'm getting out right now." I unplugged the stopper and watched as the water swirled down the drain. I grabbed my towel from the rack beside the sink and quickly dried off, slid my gown on, brushed my teeth, and opened the door. Mama was standing there glaring at me. I turned around and quickly picked up my dirty clothes that were on the floor beside the tub.

"Gina, you 'bout slow as a turtle. You better be glad I'm in a good mood or I'd whip yo'… Get out of my sight and go to bed! Lamar, you better be quick."

"Ok Mama." Lamar said as he rushed past her into the bathroom, closing the door behind him.

I was still holding my dirty clothes in my hand as I waited for Mama to move so that I could take them to the dirty clothes hamper which was located in a little room in the kitchen.

"What you standing there waitin' fo' Gina?"

"I need to put these in the dirty clothes hamper." I said raising up my arm so she could see my clothes.

"Hmmph…well hurry it up. Next time I see you it better be with yo' eyes closed and your butt in that bed."

"Yes ma'am. I'm going Mama." I quickly ran to the kitchen, dumped my dirty clothes, and hurried back to the bedroom. I jumped into the bed and slid under the covers. I was half asleep by the time Lamar came out of the bathroom.

"Nite Lamar." I said. I don't know if he replied or not because I couldn't fight the heaviness of my eyelids and drifted off into sleep.

Chapter 4
An Unforgettable Christmas

It was finally Christmas break. Even though we were poor I was still excited. Three weeks without school and I already knew that Mama had gotten us a few things for Christmas. Lamar and I stayed home each day as usual while Mama worked. He and I were getting along and I guess it was because of the fact that it was Christmas season. Lamar was excited about waking up to find toys under the tree. At eight years old he still believed that there was a Santa Claus. I didn't have the heart to burst his bubble. Although there were times when he made me angry that I thought about telling him just to be spiteful, but that wasn't who I was.

Time flew by and before we knew it, Christmas Eve had come. Before Mama met Mr. Carl I thought that it would only be the three of us for Christmas this year, but that wasn't going to happen now. While we were sitting up helping Mama bake the cake and pies, she told us that Mr. Carl would be spending the day with us. My whole mood changed, but of course I didn't let Mama see it. Why did he have to come over? Why couldn't Mama see that I wanted it just to be her, Lamar, and me?

I refused to be depressed on Christmas day. I decided to think positively and hope that something would come up and Mr. Carl wouldn't be able to come. Or if he did visit, then he would not be able to stay long. I fell asleep that night with thoughts of presents and Christmas dinner on my mind.

"Gina! Wake up!" I jumped up and hit my head on Lamar's top

bunk as Mama came into the room with her usual early morning yelling routine. She scared me half to death. It felt like I had just put my head on the pillow.

"Mama? What is it?" I asked sleepily.

"Y'all wake up. Merry Christmas!!!! Mama laughed and I swear I saw her belly shake like a bowl of jelly.

"Please, please Lord don't let her be drinking this early in the morning. It would ruin the whole day." I prayed quickly as I rolled over and sat up on the edge of my bed. The bare floor was cold to my feet. I didn't have any bedroom shoes and forgot to put socks beside the bed the night before. The bare dark brown linoleum floor felt like a cement sidewalk during a snowstorm. Not that I had ever experienced a snowstorm since I lived in the South, but I could imagine how cold it would be if there was one.

I walked across the hall to the bathroom. As I closed the door I heard Mama trying to wake Lamar up. Even on Christmas Day that boy didn't get up early. When I came out of the bathroom Lamar was sitting up in the top bunk looking like he was lost. He definitely was not a morning person. His eyes were all wild-looking and his face was all frowned up. I bet Mama didn't see that look or she would have slapped it off his face. Knowing how my brother was in the morning, I stayed quiet. I didn't want to get him started to further mess up my day. Finally, he got down and brushed past me to go into the bathroom which gave me a chance to get dressed. I had washed my face and "wiped off," as we called it, in the sink. I put on a pair of old blue jeans and a t-shirt. I could smell the bacon that Mama had cooked for breakfast. Our Christmas morning routine was to eat breakfast, clean up the kitchen, and then we could open the presents.

I was dressed and out of the bedroom before Lamar came back. I walked down the hall smiling as I saw the lights on the Christmas tree blinking. We had a pretty tree. Mama did most of the decorating and would allow Lamar and me to hang a couple of the "bulbs" as we called them. I didn't learn to call them ornaments until much later in life. The lights were different colors and blinked at different times. There were quite a few more presents under the tree than last night. My heart started to beat faster as I thought of the possibility that I missed a couple of gifts and had more under the tree. I rounded the corner to go into the kitchen and stopped dead in my tracks. I couldn't help myself. I was hoping that Mr. Carl couldn't make it, but there he was sitting at our table on Christmas morning. If only I was dreaming and this could be a nightmare! I pinched myself and closed my eyes and reopened them; only to find that he was still there. Well, there goes the day I thought to myself. Our first Christmas and we had to share it with somebody else. He was sitting at the table drinking coffee. Since I was halfway into the kitchen I had no choice but to walk in and sit down at the table. Mama had made her way back into the kitchen too and now was standing at the stove taking some store bought biscuits out of the oven. Biscuits were about the only thing I knew of that Mama couldn't make from scratch. The last time she tried to make a batch you could have broken a window with them things.

"Good morning Ginia. You ain't got manners enough to speak when you walk into the room." Mr. Carl said.

Mama whirled around and slapped me before I knew what was happening.

"Open yo' mouth when grown folk talk to you."

"Good morning Mr. Carl. Good Morning Mama." I said. My face was hurting and I could taste blood, but I refused to cry in front of this man. I already hated him. I didn't like the way he looked at me and I didn't like the fact that he couldn't say my name right. He always said it like my first name was Virginia by calling me Ginia and not Gina. He had to be illiterate I thought to myself as I sat down at the table. Lamar walked in and said good morning to everybody before he sat at the table. I saw him cut his eyes at me and smirk. Oooh…how that little boy got on my nerves and I'm sure he was somewhere peeping when Mama got on to me. My cheek was still stinging and I gently massaged it while we waited for Mama to put the food on the table. I glanced over at Mr. Carl and he was looking at me. It made me feel very uncomfortable and I looked down to see if anything was wrong with my clothes. Everything looked fine and I decided to keep my eyes away from his face for the rest of the morning.

We made it through breakfast. I sat there most of the time concentrating on my food as I listened to Mama and Mr. Carl chit-chat. I ended up washing all the dishes and putting them away while Lamar swept the floor. At least today he was made to help out.

"Gina and Lamar, y'all come on in here. It's time to open the presents!" Mama called out.

I couldn't help but smile and my heart started beating fast again. I loved Christmas time. I understood why we celebrated Christmas which was to remember the birth of Jesus, but my favorite parts were the food and presents. Lamar and I went into the living room and Mama started handing us gifts. I opened my boxes and saw my new outfits, shoes, and the watch that I had found earlier in Mama's closet. Lamar got the new shoes he wanted and was grinning like a Cheshire cat at the new outfit. It was a gray Nike jogging suit with the matching jacket. A name brand anything in our house got us excited because it was not something Mama could afford often. There were five more gifts under the table. Two of them ended up being for Mr. Carl. Mama had bought him a green sweater and some t-shirts. One of the gifts belonged to Mama and when she opened it she squealed like a kid.

"Oh Carl! Thank you honey! I love it!" She exclaimed as she wrapped herself up in a cream colored jacket that had a fur trim collar.

I looked at the collar and wondered if it was squirrel or possum because I knew he couldn't afford anything expensive, but it was a pretty jacket and looked good on Mama. Mama rarely got gifts for Christmas unless she bought it for herself and put it under the tree. Lamar and me would always make little cards and give them to her. So it was good to see her so happy as she admired the jacket. There were still two presents left. One was for me and the other was for Lamar. Mama handed them to us and I looked to see who it was from.

The name on the tag read: "From Carl." It was written in Mama's handwriting and I wondered if he could write or not. I opened the box and found a pair of dark gray gloves with the initial "G" on each one of them. Lord knows I needed these. My hands got so cold during the week when I stood outside waiting on the bus.

"Thank you Mr. Carl."

"You welcome baby."

I looked up at him and he was looking at me funny again. It made me uncomfortable and I turned my attention to Lamar. He had the same thing except his gloves were dark blue and had an "L" on them.

"Thank you Mama. I like my presents." I said smiling.

"You welcome. Mama wish she could do mo' but you know how it is Gina."

"Yes ma'am." I replied.

"Lamar, go out there and look on the front porch and bring me that cup I left out there yesterday."

"Ok, Mama."

I knew Mama was setting him up to find the new bike. This should be funny. You could hear that boy screaming like a girl.

"Thank you, thank you Mama! A new bike! I love it! Gina now you and me don't have to ride together on the same bike no mo'. He was so excited you could barely tell what he was saying.

"Mama, can I ride my new bike now?"

"Yeah, Lamar. Go on and enjoy yourself. Gina, you can go out there and ride your bike with him. Don't y'all go out in that road."

"Ok Mama." Yes! I was saying to myself because I was ready to get out of the house. I quickly ran down the hall and put away all of our presents so that the living room would be clean. I put on my shoes and ran outside. The weather wasn't too bad for a Christmas morning. Actually, it was warmer than it should have been and that made it even better. Lamar and I played outside for over an hour before we went back in the house. Well, for a day that started out horrible because of Mr. Carl, things turned out to be alright. Two of our friends, Tonya and

Kenny, came over and showed us their Christmas presents. Tonya was Kenny's big sister just as I was to Lamar. They both had gotten new bikes too. Tonya and I were in the same grade and hung out at school sometime during recess. She was kind of chubby and had short kinky hair. All of the kids picked on her about being fat and nappy headed. I took pity on her and we became friends. Kenny was Lamar's age, but he was a grade behind Lamar in school. Kenny was a little slow. He liked Lamar, but Lamar would often take advantage of him by getting Kenny to give away his toy cars or making him ask his mom for money and then Lamar would take it. I was glad to see them because they were going to be moving away right after Christmas. Tonya's mom was going to move back to South Carolina where her parents lived. I was going to miss having someone to play with and hang out with at school. We played and played until our moms called us in.

Lamar and I said goodbye to our friends and went inside. Mama told us to take a bath and if we were hungry, then we could eat some dinner. Lamar asked if he could go first for a change and I let him. Wow! I thought to myself. This indeed would be an unforgettable Christmas because Lamar wanted to bathe first and on top of that we didn't argue once all day which meant that Mama didn't have to yell at us the whole day!

Chapter 5
New Year's Eve

A week flew by so fast. It seemed like it was just Christmas day. A lot has changed since then. The worst being that Mr. Carl has moved in with us. I could not believe Mama could be so weak. She hardly knew this man and now he was living with us. I was so angry. I didn't like him. He wasn't very nice to us and he had been yelling at Lamar all week. A couple of times he had threatened to beat him, but thank the Lord Mama had the sense to step in. She told him that we were her children and she was the only one who would be beating us. It was New Year's Eve and I knew that Mama would be doing her traditional thing and going to what was called "Watch Night" services at our church. They would have church until midnight and then celebrate the coming in of the New Year. Every year Lamar and I would go with Mama and we both would be sleep by midnight, but we woke up afterwards because they would always have a big fish fry. There would also be fried chicken, collard greens, rice, pies, cakes, and all other kinds of food. Nobody cared that it was late and would eat their fill. Except for the boring sermons, I actually enjoyed going. Services always started at nine o'clock and Mama would try to get there a few minutes early. It was about seven o'clock when she came into the room where Lamar and I were playing a game of "I declare war."

"Gina, I'm goin' to church tonight. You and your brotha gonna be stayin' here with Carl."

My mouth dropped opened. I couldn't believe what I had just

heard. Lamar and I were going to stay home with Mr. Carl? He was a stranger to us. I had to say something. "Mama, I want to go." I said holding back the tears that were welling up in my eyes. What was wrong with her? Why would she leave us alone with this man that she hardly knew?

"What I say. I ain't takin' y'all. Lamar ain't got nothin' to wear and I forgot to get you some pantyhose. Y'all gonna be alright with Carl. Obey what he says. I'll be back in three hours. I ain't staying for the food this time."

"I'll be good Mama." Lamar said.

You could see the laughter on his face. He was so happy. There were two things that Lamar hated the most and that was bathing and going to church. Two hours went by like two minutes and Mama was out the door. She was wearing a dark blue suit with white piping around the sleeves and collar. She wore blue and white earrings that hung in small hoops from her ears. Her shoes were dark blue and she wore skin tone pantyhose. Mama had that suit for as long as I can remember, but she always looked good whenever she wore it. It was one of my favorite suits that she had to wear. As I watched her walk out, my heart sank a little. Lamar and I were now alone with a man we hardly knew.

Mr. Carl was sitting in the living room drinking beer and watching the TV. Lamar and I were on our way back to our rooms to play.

A few minutes after Mama left, Mr. Carl came down the hall and stood in the doorway of our bedroom. "Ginia, get your ass in there and wash them dishes."

"Mr. Carl, I already washed the dishes." I said looking up at him. He was holding a beer in one hand and a belt in the other one.

"You don't talk back to me gal. You didn't wash 'em good enough. Yo' Mama ain't here now. Get in there and do what I said."

He looked at me as if he wanted to beat me or something. I couldn't show him how much it hurt me to go in that kitchen and re-wash those dishes. So, I didn't say another word to him. I ran the dishwater and quickly washed the dishes again. I dried everything and put every dish in its place, and then I let the water out of the sink. I hurried to my room where Lamar was sitting playing with a couple of his toy cars.

"Why he make you wash the dishes over Gina?"

"I don't know Lamar. I think he's drunk or high or something."

"Yeah, maybe you right. Even I thought that was weird. You know I don't like church, but tonight I'd rather be there with Mama than be here."

"Me too. Maybe he'll drink himself to sleep. Let's stay quiet and he probably won't bother us."

"Ok." Lamar said.

I went and got onto my bed and started reading one of my favorite books, a Nancy Drew Mystery. I kept looking at my new watch and realized that only an hour had passed since Mama left. This was going to be one long night. I was just getting to a good part when Mr. Carl walked into the room again. I looked up and wondered what he wanted this time. Lamar was sitting near the window playing with his cars and he looked up to see what was going on too.

"Y'all need to go to bed," he said as he looked at me.

"Mr. Carl, Mama always let us sit up late for New Year's Eve," said Lamar as politely as I've ever heard him speak. All of a sudden it seemed like things happened in slow motion. Mr. Carl walked over to the window and snatched Lamar up off of the floor with one hand.

"Look here you little nigga! You better recognize who you talkin' to. I ain't like yo' no good daddy and them other men yo' Mama been with. I will kick your little snotty nosed ass. You don't talk to me unless I tell you to. You understand?" He sneered into Lamar's face.

I could see that Lamar had forgotten about trying to be tough. I saw the fear on his face. No man, nobody, had ever talked to him like that or treated him like that.

"I said do you understand?" Mr. Carl asked again.

"Y-y-yes sir. I understand." cried Lamar.

"Now both of y'all got ten minutes to bathe and get in the bed. From now on y'all better recognize that things have changed now that I am livin' here. I'm in charge." He finished his speech and walked back to the living room. Lamar quickly got his sleeping clothes and rushed into the bathroom to bathe first and he was out in three minutes flat. I got in and out in about the same time. I slept in t-shirt and shorts just like Lamar did. Mama promised that one day she would buy us a pair of pajamas, but that day hadn't come yet. It was about ten thirty or so when we got in the bed. I remembered thinking that Mama would be home soon and the house would feel normal again, at least as normal as it ever got for us. I decided to lie there pretending to sleep until she got home. I guess I must have fallen asleep though because sometime later something woke me up.

At first I thought I was dreaming, but it felt like someone had touched my arm and whispered my name. I opened my eyes and looked around and realized that I was not in my room. Where was I? I blinked my eyes a couple of times to focus and realized that I was in Mama's room. How did I get in Mama's room? Maybe I was dreaming.

"Ginia, are you awake?" Mr. Carl whispered.

My first impulse was to scream my head off, but I was scared. My heart started beating so loud that I could hear it myself. I felt the hairs on the back of my neck raise up. Oh Lord, what was happening? I could feel his breath on the back of my neck and his breath smelled of beer.

"Say something gal. I know you ain't sleeping. I can tell."

Maybe if I kept pretending to be asleep he wouldn't bother me and fall asleep or leave or something and I could go back to my room.

"Ginia, I know you awake gal."

I was too scared to move. Finally, I whispered, "Mr. Carl. Can I go back to my room please? Mama gonna be home soon."

"No she ain't. She called and said that she had to stay late at that church. They wanted her to help with the food. You and me got a couple of hours."

In spite of myself I started to cry. He rolled me over and put his hand over my mouth. "You better shut up." He said and I could feel his breath on my face. I could smell it too and it stank of liquor, not beer, and just plain bad breath.

"M-m-m…Mr. Carl, please don't do this!" I pleaded.

"One more word and I'll kill you." That's when I looked up and saw the glint of a knife blade in his hand. I felt as if I was going to pass out. Mr. Carl was a madman and Mama had let him into our lives.

He came close to my face holding the knife so I could see it. "After I'm done with you, then I'll go in there and kill that other little bastard of yo' Mama's and get her when she get home. You do what I say and everybody will be alright. You hear me?" he sneered.

I shook my head and tried to keep myself from making noise. God please help me I prayed. I didn't know much about adult things, but I knew that something bad was about to happen to me and there was nothing I could do about it. I cried out to God in my mind and pleaded that He would have mercy.

I felt Mr. Carl's hands moving to my shorts and I wanted to squirm and try to get away, but my body would not move. I felt sick, like I was going to throw up. His hand was trying to go inside my shorts. The tears started flowing for real. I couldn't stop him. His other hand was still covering my mouth. I whimpered and he slapped me so hard I thought I was going to pass out.

"Shut the hell up, before I kill you! Relax and you will enjoy this as much as me."

Suddenly, I heard the sound of a car door slamming in the distance, then I could faintly hear Mama telling somebody thanks for the ride. I remembered thinking that the bedroom window must have been up; otherwise you couldn't have heard anything outside. Mr. Carl must have heard everything that I did because he jumped up like he was on fire.

"Get up! Get out here and go to bed! If you say one word or I hear one sound, all of you gonna die tonight. You better not ever tell. You hear me?"

"Y-y-yes sir." I said and ran and jumped in my bed before I heard his reply. I got under the covers and turned my face to the wall. I had to calm myself down so Mama would think I was sleeping like Lamar. I heard her come in the front door.

"Hey. Carl honey. Where the kids?" Mr. Carl must have reached the living room just as Mama opened the door.

"They went to bed early. Claimed they was tired, but I think they missed you baby. Bertha, I thought you were staying late."

"I was, but I promised the kids I'd be back early. I got somebody to cover for me. Why? You not happy to see me?"

"You know I am. Come on in here and let me show you."

Mama started giggling as they went into the bedroom. I could feel the vomit rising up in my throat, but I held it down. If I threw up, then Mama would know something was wrong for sure. I believed him when he threatened to kill everybody. There was nobody I could tell. Thank God for sending Mama home early, but I had a feeling this wasn't over.

Chapter 6
Time for a Change

Six months has passed since that awful night on New Year's Eve. I tried my best to act normal, but my fear and anger had a way of showing up in other ways. In school, I had always been an "A" student, but my grades started dropping during the last nine weeks of school. By the end of the year I ended up with more "B's" than "A's." Mama fussed and cursed. She asked me what was wrong and I told her that seventh grade was really hard and I promised to do better next year. I was glad that I had passed. When I was home I made sure that I kept busy or made sure that I was outside playing with Lamar. Mr. Carl was always nice to us when Mama was around. Thank the Lord she hadn't left us alone with him since New Year's Eve. I tried to avoid eye contact with him at all times, but whenever I did look at him he would give me this dirty look. If only I could tell Mama, then she could make him go away.

It was the first day of June and Mama came in all excited. I wondered what could possibly be going on this time.

"Lamar! Gina! Come here!" She yelled.

Lamar and I ran into the living room to see what was going on.

"What is it Mama?" I asked.

"We're moving!"

"Moving?" Lamar said.

"Yeah, boy. You heard me. We gonna move into a bigger apartment. You and Gina gonna have your own rooms."

"Woohooo!!!" Lamar and I screamed and started dancing and jumping around like we had won a million bucks.

"For real Mama?" I asked.

"Yeah."

"When?!" Lamar asked excitedly.

"Next week. We have to be out of here by next Monday. So y'all got a lot of packing to do."

"Where is it Mama?"

"It's right around the corner in the projects next to the old laundry mat."

"I can't wait to have my own room." Lamar said.

"Me too."

"Mama," I said quietly, "is Mr. Carl coming too?" I stepped back because I figured I had a slap or something coming.

"No, he ain't coming. Matter of fact, he got his own place."

I almost did a cartwheel. Now that was some good news, but it didn't last long.

"You won't believe it, but he's moving to an apartment that is next door to ours. So it's gonna be just like he's still livin' with us." Mama said happily.

I almost cried, but then I wouldn't have been able to explain my tears. So I just held them inside and told myself to toughen up and focus on the fact that at least he wouldn't be in the house all the time. Maybe that thing that happened on New Year's Eve was a onetime thing and it was 'cause Mr. Carl had drank too much. I prayed to the Lord that it was over. Next week came pretty quick and my granddaddy came over to help us move. I loved my granddaddy more than life itself. He pulled up in his old white Ford pickup on the day we were moving. I was watching from the window as he got out to come up the sidewalk. Granddaddy was average height, slim, and had a full head of thick gray hair. At sixty-five years old he was still a hard worker. He had retired but he still spent most of his time doing odd jobs like shelving and painting. His skin was the color of dark chocolate because he spent so much time in the sun. My granddaddy was a good looking man for his age. If I had to point out a flaw, then it would be the fact that his ears were a little big for the size of his head and they jutted out slightly. I ran out to meet him before he reached the front door.

"Hey Granddaddy!" I said running up to give him a hug.

"Hey Dumplin', where your brotha at?" He said smiling as he hugged me back.

"He in the house packing the rest of his stuff."

My grandparents had been giving us nicknames ever since I could remember and mine was "Dumplin." My grandma said granddaddy named me "dumpling" because one summer I had ate nearly a whole pot of them that my grandma had fixed. I was so glad to see granddaddy. It seemed like forever since I had last seen him. Mama was still mad at grandma for putting her out of the house. She didn't even take us to visit for Christmas, but she did let us call them and talk on the phone every week. It just wasn't the same. Today, I decided that I would enjoy granddaddy as much as possible while he helped us move.

"And your Mama?"

"Sir?"

"I say where ya Mama?"

"She's bringing boxes to the living room."

"Well, I'm a back the truck up to da porch. You can load the light stuff."

"Ok Granddaddy."

Lamar finally came out carrying his boxes of stuff. It took a whole day to move into the new apartment. Granddaddy had to make four trips to get all of our stuff. On the final trip I sat on the back of the truck and looked at the little apartment as we drove away. I really liked the neighborhood. I didn't have many friends there, but it was still a good place. I wondered what the new neighborhood would be like. I was excited about finally having my own room even though to start off there wouldn't be much furniture in it.

We drove up to the new apartment. It was a typical project unit connected to a long row of apartments and was located on the end.

The outside was brick and it had a high cement porch with three steps. A sidewalk ran from the porch and connected to the main side walk that ran down the center of two rows of apartment buildings. The porches faced each other which meant that when you were sitting outside you would be able to talk with your neighbors and see everybody sitting on their porches. On the side of the apartment was an area without grass which was all sand. It had a big oak tree in the center of it and I figured that Lamar and I would spend many days playing there.

Mama went ahead to open the door and I jumped off the back of the truck and ran behind her. She told me and Lamar to come on in and see our rooms. I walked into the living room and saw that it was much bigger than the last apartment, but it had the same brown linoleum floor and the cement walls. Unlike the last apartment, the heater in the living room was huge. It stood right beside the door and had a huge pipe running up into the ceiling. Of course, there was no air conditioning in the projects. Either you had to buy a window unit, use an electric fan, or pray that a good breeze would blow every now and then. Mama said that she had heard that the housing people had started remodeling some of the apartments and giving them central air and heat. I guess they hadn't made it around to these projects yet, but I wished they had. Walking across the living room and to the right was a long hallway. The kitchen was to the left. There was more counter space and a bigger refrigerator that stood right beside the back door. On the wall beside the refrigerator there was a pantry for Mama to keep all of her canned goods. Continuing down the hall the first room on the right was Mama's, Lamar's room was at the end of the hall on the same side as Mama's and mine was across the hall. My room faced the back of the neighborhood. It was a nice sized room I suppose and there was a closet for me to put just my clothes. Next to my room were the bathroom and a little space for the washing machine. I liked everything and I couldn't wait to decorate my room.

We unloaded everything and put boxes in the rooms that they were supposed to be in. Granddaddy stayed awhile and talked to Mama. I think he convinced her to forgive grandma and make up. I heard her tell him that she would let us spend some of the summer with them starting next week, but he would have to come and get us. I was grinning from ear to ear as I thought of seeing grandma after all this time. She was funny and always cooked good food. I turned my attention back to unpacking my clothes and putting them into the dresser drawers. Mama had separated the bunk beds and now Lamar and me had one each in our rooms. My closet did not have a door, but Mama said that I could hang a curtain over it. After I had finished unpacking my clothes I made up my bed. I put the white cotton sheets on and then covered them with the yellow spread being careful to tuck some under the pillows. I loved to make sure my bed was made perfectly and the spread was hanging evenly on every side. Although scarce of furniture, my room looked good by the time I had finished. My dresser was beside the door as you walked in and the bed was on the wall to the right of the door with the head part against the wall. Smiling, I walked across the hall to see how Lamar was coming along.

"What you smiling for?" he asked as I walked into his room.

"I'm happy to have my own room. How 'bout you?"

Smiling he said, "Yeah, me too."

"Guess what I heard."

"What?"

"Mama told granddaddy that we could spend some of the summer with 'em." I got so excited again just by telling Lamar.

"For real?"

"Yeah...I can't wait."

"Cool. Least we won't be bored at home every day."

"You want some help?"

"Ok."

Maybe space was what we all needed I thought to myself. Lamar actually seemed civilized as we worked together to get his room organized. A lot had happened since we moved out of my grandparents' house. I was looking forward to the summer and hoping it would not pass by too fast even though I was excited to be going to high school next year. Technically, I wouldn't be in high school, but eighth grade which was called junior high. It was still exciting because they had just built a new building and decided to include seventh and eighth grade. Mr. Carl came by later and I was glad to be able to escape outside for awhile. I found out that he wouldn't be living in the apartment next door, but he was in a group of apartments over on the next block. That made me feel better because I don't know how I could have stood him living too close to us. Since things were changing for the better, maybe he and Mama would break up soon.

Chapter 7
Summer Days at Grandma's House

As we drove into the dirt lane that granddaddy considered a driveway, my grandma was sitting on the porch. Like my granddaddy, grandma also had a head full of beautiful white and gray hair, except hers was much longer. She sat in her favorite old rocking chair on the porch. She was wearing a red dress and a white apron. She was holding a large silver pan on her lap. Beside her sat a huge brown barrel and I knew that she had bought a bushel of peas to shell and put in the deep freezer. Grandma's skin was the color of coffee with two scoops of cream, at least that's how granddaddy described it whenever he told us the story of how the two of them met. She had dark colored eyes. As a matter of fact grandma's eyes were so dark that they looked black and she had the eyesight of an eagle for her age! She was average height and not fat, but plump. Although granddaddy was my favorite, I loved my grandma a lot too. As soon as the truck stopped Lamar and me got out and ran onto the porch.

"Grandma! Heyyyy! I miss you so much!" I said as I ran up the steps to hug my Grandma. Lamar wasn't far behind.

"Hey Grandma's babies! I missed y'all too. Mmmm…mmmph," she said as she hugged both of us, "Give me some sugar. How y'all been?" She kissed my cheek first and then Lamar's cheek. You would have thought Lamar and me had won the grand prize at the fair or something. We were so happy and giggling like two crazy people.

"We been good. We gotta new apartment and I got my own room. Lamar too."

"That's what ya granddaddy tole me."

"Grandma, you got some food?" Lamar asked.

"You know I do boy. I baked a choc'late cake for you and a car'mel for you Gina. For supper we gonna have fried chicken, mashed taters, gravy, biscuits, and anglish peas."

I smiled as I listened to my Grandma give us her menu for dinner. She and my granddaddy always called green peas, anglish peas and not English peas. Neither one of them had finished high school, but my Grandma could read and sign her name. Granddaddy could recognize simple words, but he didn't read or write at all.

"Mmmm…Grandma. I can't wait. That sounds good."

"Umm…hmmm," Lamar said rubbing his stomach.

"Y'all come on in here and put ya bags in the room. Y'all can watch the TV or play outside until suppertime."

Lamar and me ran and put our bags in the back room where we used to sleep when we lived with our grandparents. Then we ran outside to play. A lot of our old friends were playing ball up the road in a little grass lot that stood between two houses. We asked if we could go and play with them and grandma told us to go ahead.

"Hey Mike, John, all y'all. Can we play?" I asked as we ran onto the lot.

"Gina and Lamar! Look who's back on this side of town."

"Why Mike, it sounds like you missed us." I said smiling. Mike was the older kid in the neighborhood. He was only a year older than me though, but all the other kids looked up to him. He was a tall kid about five ten and came from a pretty decent family being that his parents were married and still together. John was Lamar's age and they had been good friends since toddlers I think. There were a few of the other neighborhood kids there, Tommy, Ricky and his brother Jim, PeeWee Johnson, and a couple of other guys. There were girls in the neighborhood, but they were all the prissy type. I was a bit of a tomboy and always loved to play with the boys.

"Nahh. We knew y'all were coming back cuz your granddaddy them still living down the street."

"Anyway, can we play?"

"Yeah. We playing the usual, two hand touch football. You still know how to play that don't you?"

"Just watch and see."

I got on the team opposite Mike's because I knew they couldn't play as well as his team. I'm not sure how long we played, but by the end of the game my team had won. Boy, did I rub it in because Mike was also a football player. Lamar and me said our goodbyes and went back to my grandparents' house. The sand felt good between my toes as we walked the short distance. The street was not paved and had been scraped and there was a layer of sand over it in which we kids loved to play in during the summer. My grandparents were not rich by any means. In fact, they were poor but always managed to stay a step ahead of being completely without.

As we walked towards my grandparent's house, I admired the simple neighborhood. Each house was unique. There was a brick one story house with green shutters about two houses up from my grandma's on the opposite side of the street. The lawn was always green and the backyard was huge with a lot of shade trees. I considered the people who lived there to be quite well-off because of the way they kept their house and yard. Other houses were either wood siding or made out of cement blocks. My grandparent's house was different all together. It was brown imitation brick with white shutters. The front of the house had two doors which I always thought was pretty cool. The front porch was high off of the ground and we kids really liked that because we could crawl under there and hide or play. There were three cement steps leading up to the porch. We opened the screen door and walked into the house.

The smell of chicken and gravy filled the air and my stomach started growling to remind me that I needed food. The living room was very large with a nice fireplace. One of the things that most people would find odd was the fact that my grandparents slept in the living room. It was large enough for them to fit two twin beds in addition to a sofa and a love seat. Mama said that they always slept like that and it had something to do with how my grandparents were used to sleeping when they were growing up.

"Gina, Lamar? That y'all?"

"Yes ma'am. We just came in from playin'." Lamar said before I could answer.

"Y'all go and wash ya hands. It's suppertime."

"Yes ma'am!" We both said in unison as we hurried to the bathroom. I couldn't wait to bite into one of Grandma's hot buttermilk biscuits and that crispy fried chicken.

We ended up spending a month of our summer vacation with my grandparents. It was the highlight of the whole summer because Lamar and me got to play with all of our old friends. More importantly, we got the chance to do all the fun things with my grandparents that we had missed out on since the fallout. They took us fishing at least twice a week. On the weekends we would spend Saturdays riding out in the country visiting friends and distant relatives of my grandma's. On Sunday we would go to church which usually ended up taking the whole day if you added the forty five minute drive there and back.

Some of my favorite memories were the times that my grandparents would take us fishing. My grandparents knew a white man, Mr. Nix, who owned a cabin in the mountains. Granddaddy usually did work for him during the summer and he would let my grandparents stay in his cabin whenever they wanted to. Whenever they went, Lamar and I usually tagged along with them. A small stream ran behind the cabin and granddaddy would usually go trout fishing whenever we went there. Sometimes Lamar and I would fish, but mostly we just liked to play and enjoy watching our grandparents while they fished. If I wasn't fishing or playing with Lamar, then I would spend my time daydreaming. I always thought how peaceful it was sitting there watching the little stream flow over the rocks. The days spent with my grandparents were some of the best days of my life as a kid.

Chapter 8
A Life-Changing Moment

The summer before I started junior high flew by really fast. There were only two days left before school started. Lamar and I had about three new outfits each to start off. Mama still had to find me some shoes. The money was very tight this year, but I really needed some new shoes. The next day Mama went downtown to the dollar store and found me a ten dollar pair of shoes. They were kind of like the shoes that boaters wore casually, but you could tell that they were cheap. The color was a yellowish-brown and the shoe was flat with no kind of heel. When Mama brought them home, I said thanks and took them to my room. Later that night as I sat on my bed looking at the shoes sitting in my closet, I cried like a baby. I was about to start junior high and on the first day of school I would have to wear those ugly, cheap shoes. I could already hear the jokes, "Gina, where'd you get them shoes? The flea market? Naww, she got 'em from a yard sale." Tears kept streaming down my face. Lord, help me to be strong and not worry about what the kids at school would say. I should be thankful that at least I had shoes to wear.

It was now the day before school was to start and Mama had to do my hair. I had some thick, kinky hair and it was all natural. Mama was scared to put any type of chemicals in it, because she couldn't afford for somebody else to do it and she had no clue on how to relax hair which she proved the time that she tried to do my hair. Actually, my hair came out nappier after the relaxer than it was before she started. Thank the Lord my hair didn't come out. I was able to take some vinegar and eggs and wash the relaxer out. My hair was so hard and kinky afterwards that I could barely comb it. Mama promised she'd never try that again and I was thankful.

"Gina! Come on in here so I can do that nappy head of yours!" Mama yelled from the kitchen.

"Yes Ma'am!" I yelled back as I picked up a book to read. Mama had already washed my hair earlier in the day and let it air dry before pressing it out. It was a typical August day and it was very hot outside. Mama had the window air conditioner on in her room, but you really couldn't tell it. The rest of the apartment was just as hot as it was outside. I prayed that my hair would at least hold up for the first day of school. I walked into the kitchen and sat down in the chair by the stove where Mama had the straightening comb heating up. Mama had sectioned my hair into small plaits so that it could dry faster. She took the first one loose and combed through it.

"Ouch! That hurt!"

"Look, don't you start Gina. You ought to be used to this by now. Hold your head still if you want me to do your hair. I ain't got all day."

I was what they called tender-headed and Mama was by no means gentle as she combed through my hair with that pressing comb. It took her about two hours to finish. One thing I could say about Mama and pressing hair, she was good at it. When she finished my hair was slick to my head. There wasn't a nap in sight as I looked in the mirror. Mama styled my hair with a pony tail in the front and the back was curled up. It looked really good as I stood there smiling at myself. The rest of the evening came and went and it was soon time to get ready for bed. I was a little excited as I thought about being back at school the next day and seeing all of my old classmates. I had ironed a pair of blue jeans that had a boot leg cut. They had a pink flower on the right leg and I was going to wear a light pink baby doll top with them. The outfit would have been real cute if I had matching shoes, but I didn't and would have to wear what I had. Oh well, it was better than nothing I thought to myself. My window fan was blowing out hot air as I crawled between the covers, but at least it was blowing something. Maybe my hair would hold up and tomorrow would be a good day. I laid my head on the pillow thinking of my first day of junior high.

"Gina! Time to get up! You awake?"

My heart was beating hard against my chest. I was sleeping really hard when Mama came into the room that morning. Why in the world did she have to yell out of the blue like that?

"Wake up Gina."

"I'm awake Mama."

"You need to go on and freshen up, then get dressed and get something to eat from the kitchen."

"Yes ma'am." I said. I was still in a daze from being awakened so abruptly. Somehow I managed to sit up on the edge of the bed and finally stand up and drag myself to the bathroom. I flipped on the light to use the toilet. I stood up to wash my hands and finally looked into the mirror. Oh my God! My hair! I had a mini afro sitting on my head. It didn't even look like Mama had put any heat in it. There was no way that I could show up at school looking like this. The tears welled up in my eyes, but I refused to cry. I had to think fast. I would just have to ask Mama if I could run a lightly warmed hot comb through it again. Maybe that would work or at least hold it for the first day and then I could get some braids to finish out the rest of the week. I ran down the hall to the kitchen where Mama was still fixing breakfast.

"Mama?"

"What is it Gina?"

"I sweated out my hair last night. Can I go over it just a little bit with the hot comb?" Please Lord let her be in a good mood this morning. Let her say yes.

"I reckon. Don't burn yo' hair out and don't be thinking this gonna be a habit."

"Yes ma'am. Thank you Mama." I would have hugged her, but Mama wasn't the affectionate type with me. I got out the hot comb and put it on one of the back burners that Mama wasn't using. I let it heat up just a little bit and ran back to the bathroom. I re-pressed my hair enough for it to look good for school that day. Thank you Lord I said as I looked in the mirror at myself and smiled. I wasn't too bad looking, but I didn't think that I was cute or pretty either. My complexion was what you might call a pecan tan. My eyes were dark brown and slightly slanted, but not as much as Asian people or nothing like that. Although, kids would tease me at times about my eyes and say I looked like a Chinese. My nose was broad, but not to the point of being noticeable. I looked at my lips and was thankful that they were full and not too big. I was tall for my age and on the skinny side. I must have had a high metabolism because I loved to eat and ate a lot at times, but didn't gain any weight. Two of my best features were my hair and my smile. I had shoulder length, thick, black hair and a smile that could brighten anybody's day including my own.

"Gina!"

"Yes, Mama?"

"If you want to eat sumpt'n, you better get in here now."

"Ok."

Mama had cooked bacon, grits, and eggs. She was taking toast out of the oven as I walked into the kitchen. Lamar was already at the table. He looked quite handsome in his khaki pants and blue and white plaid button up shirt. He was wearing a plain pair of black tennis shoes. Mama had taken him down to the barber shop on Saturday for a haircut. My brother was a good-looking guy, especially when he dressed up. I sat at the table and waited for Mama, so that we could bless the food and eat. We quickly ate our breakfast and grabbed our backpacks. Lamar's school was only a block away from the apartment, but I had to catch the bus to get to my school. Mama walked Lamar to school and I headed for the bus stop which was a couple of blocks away. I was excited to be going to junior high and couldn't wait to see everybody. When I got to the bus stop I saw some kids that I knew and started talking with them until the bus arrived. Everyone was talking about the great summer that they had and all of the cool places that they had visited. I smiled and listened. One day I was going to be able to go places and see different things. The bus soon came and we all piled on. I sat with a girl named Cheryl who lived in my old neighborhood. We chatted until the bus pulled up at the school.

I got off the bus and headed in the direction of my homeroom. It was both scary and exciting to see all of the older kids walking around. This should be an interesting school year I thought to myself. I found my classroom easily, because Mama, Lamar, and me had come to visit the school a couple of weeks ago and I already knew who my homeroom teacher was going to be. Mrs. Jamison had been teaching for over 30 years and had even taught Mama. I walked into the classroom and she was sitting behind her desk reading something. She wore her hair in an afro. It was kind of a reddish gray. I guess she dyed it or something. She wasn't fat, but kind of plump. I walked over to say good morning.

"Good morning Mrs. Jamison. My name is Gina Jones."

"Well, good morning Gina. Welcome to my homeroom. I've already assigned desks and yours is right over there," she said as she pointed to a desk on the front row on the left side of her desk.

"Thank you." I said as I walked over to sit down.

The rest of the day was uneventful for a first day of school. I had to change classes four times and got to meet my different teachers. All of them seemed pretty nice, especially since no one gave us homework on the first day. I was glad when the bell rang at the end of the day. When I finally got home, Mama was hanging out clothes in the backyard. Lamar was on the side of the apartment riding his bike.

"Hey Mama. Hey Lamar."

"Hey," Lamar said.

Mama spoke and kept on hanging out the clothes. I decided to go inside and change clothes before coming back outside to play with Lamar. I walked into the apartment and was just about to turn down the hall and almost bumped into Mr. Carl. I screamed.

"Gina! What the hell is wrong with you?!" Mama said as she bustled into the kitchen.

"Nothing Mama. I didn't know Mr. Carl was in here. He scared me, that's all."

"Calm down Bertha baby. The gal didn't see me. We both came round the corner at the same time."

"Well, she don't need to be doing all that." Mama mumbled as she turned and walked back outside grumbling to herself.

I turned around and saw that Mr. Carl hadn't moved and was still blocking my way down the hall. I kept my eyes down and tried to go around him. His hands came out to stop me.

"Can't you speak Ginia? Or the cat got your tongue?"

"Hey Mr. Carl." I said quickly without looking up. "Can I please get by?"

"Hey Mr. Carl. Can I please get by?" he mimicked. "I'll let you by when you look at me."

I could feel my fist forming into a ball at my sides. My heart started pounding in my chest. I slowly looked up at him. I couldn't stand to look in his face. I didn't like the way he looked at me. He was looking at me with a half smile on his face. I just could see the glimpse of his gold tooth. If I only had the strength, I would have beaten the life out of him.

"Now, that's better. Ginia, you better start getting used to seeing me. I ain't been around lately, but that's about to change. That sho' is a pretty little outfit you wearing."

Before I could react, he had placed his hand on my shoulder. My stomach tightened into a knot at his touch. He slowly started tracing a finger from my shoulder down my chest. I went to step back and he grabbed me and pulled me up against him. He grabbed my breast and squeezed it so hard I wanted to cry.

"You better not say a word about this. Remember what I told you the last time. Yep, the time is coming soon. You and me gonna have some fun and it ain't nothing yo' mama or anybody is gonna do about it."

He let me go and walked through the kitchen and out of the door. I ran to my room and closed the door, locking it behind me. I fell on my bed and cried into the pillow. This was so wrong. Lord, why was this happening to me? I needed to do something to stop Mr. Carl. I was not going to keep quiet. My anger rose up so fast it felt like my head was going to explode. I got off of my bed and ran down the hall to go outside. Mama was just hanging up the last few pieces of clothing. She was alone. Mr. Carl must have gone home to his own apartment.

"Mama." I said breathlessly and the tears started flowing down my face.

"Gina, what's the matter with you? You can't be still scared."

"No ma'am." I was crying harder. "I n-n-eed to t-t-tell you something about Mr. Carl."

"What?"

"He grabbed me in the hall just then and touched my breast."

"You lying to me Gina?"

"No Mama. It's not the first time either. That time you went to church New Year's Eve, he carried me to your bed and was gonna rape me, but you came home." I couldn't stop long enough to catch a breath and everything flowed out at once. I had to tell her everything while I had the courage.

"What?! How come this is the first time you telling me this?"

"H-h-he said he would kill you and Lamar. Mama, I'm scared of him! He says he is gonna do bad things to me!"

"Like what?" Mama asked. Her eyes drew into narrow slits and I swore I could see her nostrils flaring.

"Bad things Mama. Things that grown ups do."

Mama let out a string of curse words. Some that I'd heard before and some that I'd dare not repeat. "Gina, don't you worry. I'll take care of this. Don't you tell nobody. You hear me?"

"Yes Mama." I finally exhaled in one long breath. I wished she had come and hugged me and told me how much she loved me and would take care of me, but she didn't. She just turned back around and kept hanging out clothes.

I felt a little better by telling Mama everything, but I was still scared that Mr. Carl was going to hurt us. He came back over to the house later that evening and he and Mama were sitting in the kitchen talking. Lamar and me were in his room playing tic-tac-toe.

"Gina, come here!" Mama called out.

I hurried down the hall to see what she wanted.

"Come on in here and sit down."

I sat down making sure to keep my eyes away from Mr. Carl's face.

"Gina, tell Carl what you told me this evening."

My head snapped up as I looked at Mama with pleading eyes. I couldn't believe she was going to make me say everything over again, especially in front of Mr. Carl. I started trembling so bad the table was shaking.

"Well gal. What lies you been telling yo' Mama about me?"

Now I got angry again because he thought I was too scared to talk. "They ain't lies! It's all true! You touched my breast today and you tried to rape me back in January!" Tears welled up in my eyes, but I wouldn't let him see me cry. I couldn't stand to look at him and found a spot on the wall to focus on that was above Mama's head.

"Carl, baby is that true?"

"Bertha, you gonna believe this little heifer of yours over me? She ain't liked me since the first time I set foot in your house. I told you that."

"Carl, I know Gina. I believe her. I promised myself that if any man ever touched my daughter, I'd kill him. You better tell me the truth right now."

"Don't play that innocent act Bertha. You told me I could." Mr. Carl said with a sneering tone. I looked at Mama and saw her face twist in anger.

"You liar! I ought to kill you Carl!" She yelled and spit flew out of her mouth.

The anger on her face looked real, but I couldn't believe what I was hearing. Did Mama really say that? Did she tell him that he could mess with me? Or was Mr. Carl just saying that to make me think Mama was on his side? Oh Lord, tell me I'm dreaming. I was angry and scared. I was too scared to move or say anything.

Mr. Carl stood up and glared down at Mama. "Bertha, if you ever raise your voice to me like that again, you'll regret it. You can pretend if you want, but we both know what the deal is."

I had no idea what that meant, but Mama recoiled as Mr. Carl stood over her. Her facial expression changed from anger to fear. She started crying. I couldn't believe this was happening. What did he mean? Why was she crying?

"Carl, baby. I'm sorry. Gina, forget this ever happened. You don't have to worry about anything like this again. Right Carl?"

"Yeah, right."

"Gina, go on back to your room."

And just like that I got up and ran down the hallway to my room. I sat there on the bed trying to figure out what had just happened. I had no idea. I didn't want to believe that Mama was so weak that she would give Mr. Carl permission to molest me. I still wasn't sure if she believed me or not. I hoped Mama would come to her senses and break up with him after learning what he had done to me. Lamar must have known that things were pretty serious because he didn't even come over to find out what was happening. I don't know how long I sat on the bed in the dark, but I finally got up and put on my nightgown. I could still hear the muffled voices of Mama and Mr. Carl in the kitchen. Lamar had gone to bed over an hour ago. I lay there waiting to hear the backdoor open and close as an indication that Mr. Carl had left, but I dozed off to sleep. I'm not sure how long I had been asleep, but something woke me up. My heart started pounding as I realized that someone was in my room. I could smell the beer on his breath. Mr. Carl had sneaked into my room somehow and was on top of me. My nightgown had been pushed all the way up and he was sucking on my breast. I can't believed I had slept that soundly. I tried to squirm out of the way, but he held me down.

"Ginia, you better not move or make a sound. Next time you tell yo'

Mama something, you really gonna have something to tattle about. Don't think that you can scream and she'll come in here. I made sure that I got her good and drunk. She'll be out until in the morning. You and me gonna have some fun."

Lord, dear Lord. Please God, don't let this happen again. Tears flowed down my face, but no sound came out of my mouth. He kept touching my breasts and putting his mouth all over them. He reached down and put his hands inside of my underwear and started touching my innermost parts. I couldn't have screamed if I had wanted to. My fear was too great that he might kill me and everybody else. I should have kept my mouth shut and maybe he would have left me alone. I prayed for it to be over. I realized that my life would never again be the same. My innocence was gone and so was my childhood. I whimpered and he slapped me hard across the face. As he started to tear into me the pain became so bad that I couldn't bear it and I blacked out. I don't know how long I was out, but when I regained consciousness he was gone. My entire body ached and I felt sticky all over. My gown was torn and my underwear was gone. Mr. Carl was standing beside the bed getting dressed and I slid across to the other side in fear. Tears were streaming down my face as I stood there in the dark, praying that he would just go away.

He started laughing. "If you breathe a word about this, I'll make you wish you were never born Ginia. I'll make your fat ass Mama and that little bastard across the hall suffer if you tell anyone. You hear me?"

"Yes." I said through clenched teeth. God help me, I wanted to kill him. I wanted to cut his lifeless heart out. My entire body hurt and I was trembling all over, but the physical pain did not outweigh the mental and emotional trauma that I felt as I stood there trying to figure out what to do. Mr. Carl turned, opened my door and walked out as if nothing had happened.

Chapter 9
The Accident

Four years have passed since that horrible night that Mr. Carl took away my innocence. In that single moment, he stripped me of my identity. I was left without self-esteem or any feeling of self-worth. I felt dirty, ashamed, and guilty. I knew that I should have called the police or my grandparents and told them everything, but I didn't. The fear of everyone knowing what happened to me and Mr. Carl's threat was more powerful than the need to punish Mr. Carl for what he had done. Even worse, Mama would have done nothing to defend me. As a matter of fact, after that night, every opportunity that she could find to belittle me and put me down she would do it. Gradually, I learned not to show any emotion about anything. I refused to show any weakness in front of her, Lamar, or Mr. Carl. After about the fifth time of Mr. Carl coming into my room, I decided that it was time to fend for myself. I began locking my bedroom door at night and pushing my dresser behind it. I even slept with a butcher knife under my pillow. I was determined to kill him if he ever touched me again. Each time Mama would curse me until she could no longer think of words to say and then she would beat me. Still I did not give in and I figured the beatings were a much better option than being raped.

My junior high years and my first two years of high school had flown by. I barely remembered anything that occurred over the last four years. It felt like my life had been on autopilot and I had gone through the motion of living each day. By the time I reached sixteen I was broken emotionally and spiritually. It had been my plan to stay a virgin until my wedding day, but now that dream had been destroyed along with so many others. It seemed that the God I had discovered at the age of five one Sunday morning at my grandparent's church had turned his back and walked away. The prayers that I had prayed and the crying that I had done in private had not protected me from the trauma that I had experienced at the hands of Mama and Mr. Carl. My personality changed after that night and even the kids at school noticed. The ones who used to pick on me and called me names soon realized that I wasn't their punching bag anymore. I began to fight back. Not physically, but I learned to use my tongue as my weapon of defense. By the time I was in high school, I could make the toughest kid cry with my harsh jokes. I became distant and bitter towards everything and everybody.

I became a loner both at school and at home. As each day passed I would sink lower and lower into my abyss of shame, guilt, and self-pity. I was now a junior in high school. All the other girls were dreaming about going to the prom in the spring. I had no expectations and no goals, but life has a way of moving on whether you actively take part or not.

"Gina!"

"Yes Mama?"

"Open this door!"

My thoughts had been interrupted as usual as I was sitting on my bed writing in my journal. I quickly tucked my journal into my secret hiding place which was a small space behind my top dresser drawer. I can't remember why, but somewhere between ninth and tenth grade I had begun keeping a journal of my thoughts and about everything that happened. It was the only way that I could express my thoughts and feel some type of emotional release.

"Gina!"

"I'm coming." I said as I walked the short distance from my bed to the door. I opened the door and Mama stood there looking like she was about to explode. I knew she didn't like me locking my door, but once she realized that beating me didn't stop me from doing it, she left me alone.

"I need you to go to the store for me. I don't have any sugar to make tea for dinner. So run around the corner to Miss Nia's little store and get a bag of sugar. Here is five dollars and I want all my change back."

"Yes ma'am." I took the money and went out the back door. Miss Nia's little store was only a block away. I would later learn that it would be similar to what became known as convenience stores. It only took me about five minutes to get there. Miss Nia was sitting in her usual spot behind the counter reading the local newspaper. The little bell hanging over the screen door rang as I walked in. Miss Nia looked up and nodded her head at me as I walked in and headed for the aisle where the sugar was located. Miss Nia must have been about seventy or so, but it was hard to tell. She was wearing a faded yellow sweater that had been crocheted and a wide color white blouse underneath. Her skin was not very wrinkled and she always wore a wig that was dyed auburn. She had the complexion that looked like dark brown sugar. Miss Nia was about average height and had kept her body in pretty good shape. She wasn't plump and everything was still hanging in its right place. As a matter of fact, if I didn't know that she had kids over fifty and could see that grey hair peaking from under the edge of her wig, I would have thought that she was a little over fifty herself. She was always nice whenever Lamar and me would come into the store and she'd give us a cookie or some candy as we were leaving. I was so absorbed in my thoughts that I did not notice someone was walking down the sugar aisle until we collided.

"S-s-sorry." I stammered as I looked up at the person that I'd bumped into. I found myself staring into warm, dark brown eyes.

"No problem. I wasn't watching where I was going either." he said.

He was a bit taller than me. His skin was the color of milk chocolate I'm sure. He had one of the nicest smiles I'd ever seen in a guy. He was also one of the most handsome boys I'd seen in awhile.

"It's ok." I mumbled and walked passed him. Calm down girl I told myself. Why had my heart began beating faster? I put the sugar on the counter and Miss Nia rang me up. My hand was shaking as I gave her the five dollar bill. She gave me my change and I walked out of the store and headed home.

"Hey!"

I turned around to see who was speaking. It was the guy that I had bumped into. He was jogging to catch up with me. I don't know why I waited, but I stood still until he was standing beside me.

"Yes?" I asked as he stood looking at me and catching his breath.

"Mind if I walk with you? I see you are going in the same direction that I am headed in.

"That's not a good idea. First of all, I don't know you. Secondly, that makes you a stranger and I'm not supposed to talk to strangers."

"Whoa!," he said with a slight frown on his face. "I'm sorry. I didn't mean to offend you. I understand if you can't walk with me. At least let me introduce myself and the next time we meet I won't be a stranger. I'm Sebastian." He extended his hand towards me and smiled.

I hesitated a moment and slowly extended my hand to meet his. "I'm Gina." I said as I shook his hand and felt myself smiling. I quickly took my hand out of his and told him that I wasn't allowed to socialize with boys because my Mama was really strict. He said that he understood and crossed over to the other side of the street. As I was turning left at the end of the block to go home, he turned right and began jogging in the opposite direction.

I wondered who he was because I had never seen him before. He seemed like a nice guy. I thought about what he said before telling me his name. He said that next time we meet we wouldn't be strangers. I doubt that would ever happen because it was obvious that he didn't live around here and I hadn't heard about any new family moving into town lately. If my life and attitude towards myself would have been different, I may have thought about him more, but I had no interest in the opposite sex. I figured that they were all rotten to the core and I wanted nothing to do with them. I didn't even care for my own gender too much because most females were either shallow and weak or snobby and naïve. I could see the apartment just ahead and began to speed up my steps. As I got closer, I could see Mama standing on the back porch with her arms folded and a nasty look on her face. Oh God. I knew that look. I searched my brain to try to figure out if I had not done something she'd told me to do. No, I did all of my chores before I left and had been sitting in my room writing in my journal. I glanced at my watch and realized that it had taken me twenty minutes to run a ten minute errand. Had I been walking that slowly? How long did I stay in the store?

"Gina! Where in the hell you been?! I've been waiting ten minutes!"

I began walking up the steps towards her. "Mama, I was hurrying as fast as I—

I didn't get the chance to finish the sentence. Her hand came out so fast I couldn't avoid it. She slapped me so hard I missed a step and stumbled backwards off of the porch. Everything went black.

"Gina? Gina? Oh Lord, what have I done?"

"Mama, Gina dead?"

Why was Lamar crying? Mama sounded as if she was crying too. I tried to open my eyes, but my head was hurting so badly I could barely think straight. Everything went black again.

I am not sure how much time had passed, but when I woke up again I heard voices whispering and the sound of something beeping in my right ear. My head was still hurting like crazy.

"Gina? Can you hear me?"

Someone was calling my name, but I couldn't speak. My head was pounding and it felt like something was holding my arms down.

"Gina. Are you awake? I am Dr. Mollier. If you can hear me, then squeeze my hand."

A doctor? Where did he come from? I could barely feel someone taking my hand. It felt like cobwebs were in my head as I tried to remember how to squeeze a hand.

"Good job, Gina. Now, can you open your eyes? Don't be afraid. There are no lights on. We don't want the bright lights to hurt your eyes."

Slowly, I managed to open my eyes and once they focused I could see the doctor standing on my right. Was I lying in a hospital room? Why?

"Good job. Well, young lady you've given everybody quite a scare. How are you feeling?"

I tried to answer and started coughing. The doctor put a cup up to my mouth and I sipped some water through the straw.

"My head is hurting." I whispered.

"That's normal after having a concussion. Do you remember what happened?"

"No, sir."

"Can you tell me how old you are?" he asked.

"I'm fourteen, no I mean sixteen. "I said as I searched my brain for the answer. It felt like a thick fog had found its way inside my brain as I tried to remember my age.

"Good girl." said Dr. Mollier. "Now do you remember your birthdate?"

"Umm. It's, it's April 10th." I whispered.

"Well, it seems that only your short term memory has been affected by the accident."

My head was pounding harder and I figured that was a direct result of trying to remember my age and birthdate. "What happened to me?"

"Well, you had an accident. Your mother told me that you lost your footing and fell down some steps at home. You hit your head on the sidewalk and passed out."

"When?"

"A couple of days ago."

"Two days? Have I been in here two days?"

"Yes. You are very lucky Gina. When you are feeling better and can remember what happened, I would like to talk to you some more. I have a few concerns about your accident, but I am going to wait until you can start remembering some of what happened. You will have to stay here a couple of more days before you can go home."

"Why?"

"We had to put some stitches in. You cracked your skull in the back. We want to monitor you for a few more days and make sure that you are recuperating."

"Where's my Mama?" I realized that should have been the first question out of my mouth. I wondered if Dr. Mollier had noticed that or not.

"She has been here with you since the ambulance brought you in through the emergency center. Your mother went to pick up your brother from school and will be back in a few hours. I don't think she was expecting you to wake up so soon."

"Oh." I was still groggy and felt myself falling asleep.

"I'll let you get some rest young lady. I'll be back to check on you later."

I barely heard Dr. Mollier's words as I drifted off. The next time I opened my eyes Lamar was standing by the bed looking at me.

"Gina? Mama, she woke up."

"Gina, you awake?" Mama asked matter-of-factly. I would have been shocked into a coma probably if I had heard any motherly concern in her voice.

"Yes ma'am."

"Well, good. I ain't think you'd wake up again. That doctor talked to you yet? What he say to you?"

"Yes Mama. He talked to me a little. I didn't say anything. He asked me some questions to test my memory and asked how I was feeling. He told me that I fell down and hit my head and that's all."

"Yeah. You so clumsy. Why you have to fall and put me through all of this? What did you tell that doctor?" she asked again as she walked closer to the bed. I could see in her eyes that she was worried about me talking to Dr. Mollier. I didn't understand why.

"Nothing Mama. I don't remember what happened."

"What?!"

"I don't remember how I fell. I didn't even know that two days had gone by."

Mama actually looked relieved and again I wondered why she was behaving so oddly. It's funny I thought to myself. I can remember all the other horrible stuff that happened to me, but my brain couldn't recall how I had fallen and hit my head. The doctor said that my memory could come back anytime. I was hoping that it would because I wanted to know why I ended up in a hospital.

"Gina. I was so scared. You was laying on the sidewalk and all that—"

"Shut up Lamar! She don't need to hear that now. Gina, you just rest. I called yo' school and yo' teachers sent some work home for you once you better."

'Thanks, Mama."

"Do you remember anything befo' the accident?"

"The accident is the only thing I don't remember." I said as I looked into my Mama's face. I could see it in her eyes that she was hoping my entire memory of the past had been wiped out. What was she thinking? We could start over or something? Did she think that she could get rid of her guilt that easily?

"Well, I'm glad you finally awake. I need to get your brotha home. He got homework. I'll be back up here tomorrow. You get some rest."

"Yes ma'am." I watched as they walked out of the door and into the hall. I lay there thinking about the brief conversation between Mama and me. She didn't even ask me how I was feeling. There was no motherly concern at all. It almost sounded as if she either wished I didn't wake up ever again or I would have complete memory loss. Tears stung my eyes as I thought about my life. My Mama didn't even love me. Lying in that hospital room with only the sound of the IV machine beeping, I realized how alone I was in the world. Even my grandparents couldn't have filled the void that I felt in my heart. I closed my eyes and prayed like never before. Although I still didn't understand why all the terrible things had happened to me, I still prayed. I told God that I was sorry for thinking that he had turned away from me. I poured my heart out to God and cried until there were no more tears to come. I fell asleep hoping that God had heard my prayer.

Chapter 10
Life or Death Decision

The two days in the hospital went by kind of fast. On the last day, the doctor came in and again asked me about the accident. I had gained my memory back by then and knew exactly what happened. He told me that he was a bit confused as to how I fell on the back of my head if I was going down the steps. Mama had told him that I lost my footing when I was going down the steps. He also mentioned the bruise on my face that didn't look like it happened in the fall. I stuck to the story that Mama had told him. I could tell that he was skeptical about the whole thing, but he didn't press the matter. Mama came to pick me up from the hospital in Mr. Carl's old beat up Ford truck. It was dark green with white-walled tires. Only three people could sit in the front comfortably. On the way home Mama didn't say one word to me and I was glad to have the silence. When we got home Lamar was sitting on the front porch. He ran down the steps and came up to my side of the truck.

"Gina! I'm glad you home. How you feelin'?"

"Better," I said as I got out of the truck, "You miss me?"

"Maybe."

Lamar was grinning as he said maybe and helped me up the porch and into the apartment. I wondered what came over him. I had never seen him act this nice before. I was feeling a little light headed and told Mama that I was going to my room to rest.

"You been laying up in the hospital for two days. Don't think you coming here and stay in the bed. First thing you gonna do is wash them dishes, then you can lay down."

"Mama, I feel dizzy and my head still hurts," the doctor said.

"I know you ain't talking back to me Gina. I don't care if yo' head hurt. As long as you live under my roof, you gonna do as I say. You ain't gonna come here and lay up thinkin' I'll wait on you hand and foot. This ain't the hospital and I sho' as hell ain't no nurse. You hear me?"

I quickly replied that I did and walked up the steps into the apartment. I could see the sink full of dishes from the doorway. My head was pounding and I felt unsteady on my feet. I didn't know Lamar was standing right behind me and he put out his hand on my back as I swayed. I looked back and saw that Mama had sat down on the porch.

I wasn't the least bit surprised that she showed me no mercy. Mama and I had no kind of relationship. As far as she was concerned I was like a live-in maid that worked without pay.

"Thanks Lamar." I said as he followed me into the kitchen. I leaned on the sink for support and began running water into it to wash the dishes. I squeezed a little of the dish detergent in the water and watched as the foam begin to spread across the sink. My head kept hurting. Another wave of dizziness swept over me. I waited until it had passed and quickly washed all of the dishes that had been left. I wiped down the stove and the countertops. Finally, I wiped off the table and hung the dish cloth over the sink. I turned around too fast and stumbled backwards into the counter. The edge of it caught me in the back. Mr. Carl was standing in the doorway of the kitchen watching me.

"Well. Look who's home. How you Ginia?" he sneered as he walked towards me. I felt the edge of the countertop digging into my back as I stood watching him. I knew that he wanted me to be afraid of him, but I wasn't. I stood up straight and met his stare head on.

"Do you really care Mr. Carl?" I said as he stopped a couple of feet in front of me. He was wearing a white t-shirt and khaki shorts. He must have been in Mama's room sleeping when we came home.

"I see you still got that smart mouth. You don't sass me gal, you hear?"

"I ain't scared of you no more Mr. Carl."

"Is that right? What makes you so brave all of a sudden?"

"I know—."

"Carl baby! Can you come out here for a minute ?" Mama was calling out from the front porch.

"Coming Bertha," he turned and was gone as quickly as he had appeared.

I didn't realize I had been holding my breath until all of the air rushed out of me. I was shaking and felt like I was about to faint. I quickly walked down the hall, leaning on the walls for support, entered my bedroom and closed the door and locked it behind me. I took two of the painkillers the doctor gave me at the hospital. I fell asleep within a few minutes.

Loud voices woke me up out of a deep, drug-induced sleep. It took me a minute to remember that I was at home. What in the world was happening? I sat up in the bed listening in the dark. It was Mama and Mr. Carl. I was used to them arguing, especially when they had been drinking. I suppose tonight was one of those nights.

"Carl, please. Please don't leave me. I need you!" I heard Mama begging.

"Let me go Bertha! Get off of me! I'm tired of you and yo' no good kids. I am through! Finished!"

"Carl, I'll do anything! Anything! Please, just tell me what you want!"

"I don't want nothing from you no mo'. You all used up Bertha."

"There's Gina. I'll make her be good to you!"

"She ain't no good to me now." He laughed, "She ain't sweet and tender like she was four years ago."

My heart pounded in my ears and my head started back hurting. Vomit rose up in my throat and I gagged. If I had never believed it before, it was all clear now. Mama had known all along what he had done to me and she had played a part in it. I jumped out of my bed and ran to my door. I lost all sense of caution as I flung the door open and ran into the hallway. Mama and Mr. Carl were at the far end facing each other. They both turned to look at me.

"Mama, how could you?! Why did you let him rape me over and over again?! How could you do that to me? I'm your own flesh and blood! What kind of mother are you?!

"Shut up! You don't know nothing Gina. You don't know how hard it is to raise two kids by yo'self. How you think we was gonna make it?!"

At that moment I didn't care what happened to me. I was tired of carrying the burden of guilt. I was outraged. "You are nothing to me Mama! Nothing!" I yelled. I was so mad I was crying. Mr. Carl was looking at me and laughing.

"Look at her Bertha. She got more spirit than you'd ever have. She got more everything than you."

Mama must have lost her mind at that moment because all I heard was a growl and the next thing I saw was Mr. Carl's body slamming into the wall as Mama charged him. He lost his footing and fell to the floor with Mama falling on top of him. Mama was fighting like a man. She was getting the best of him until he turned and she fell off of him. By this time Lamar had come out of his room. Mr. Carl got on top of Mama and started punching her in her stomach and in her face. She went from cursing to crying. He kept hitting her. The next thing I knew Lamar was standing in the hall with Mama's gun. I screamed and Mr. Carl turned around and saw Lamar pointing the gun in his face.

"Get off of my Mama." His voice was low and deep. He was aiming the gun at Mr. Carl and his arm was so calm.

"Well, well. Look at this little nigga. What you gonna do boy?"

"Kill you if I have to. Get off of my Mama."

Lamar aimed over Mr. Carl's head and fired a shot. Mama screamed and the last thing I saw before I ran into my bedroom was Mr. Carl running for the door. I could hear Mama talking on the other side of my door.

"Lamar, baby. Give Mama the gun."

"Mama, all these years, I wondered why you put up with him. I wondered why you let him beat me like he did. I never knew he messed with my sistah. You let him do things to Gina?" Why Mama? How could you?

"Lamar, son—"

"Don't son me."

There was a brief moment of silence. Then I heard Mama speak again and I could tell by the sound of her voice that she was mad enough to beat Lamar. "What you know Lamar? You ain't but twelve years old. You don't know nothing. Don't you smart mouth me boy"

"I'm sorry Mama, but…"

"Shut up! What I do is my business Lamar. You ain't got nothing to say about what I do and what go on in my house. Now give me that gun."

"I'm sorry Mama." He was so weak. I thought he was going to finally stand up for something, but he didn't. He didn't need to apologize to her. I cracked the door and I could see Mama standing in front of Lamar. She looked furious. Blood was streaming down her face and her hair was flying everywhere. The look in her eyes would have stop a criminal in his tracks. I saw it coming before Lamar did. She slapped him hard across the face.

"Don't you ever pull a gun on nobody! What's wrong with you?!"

"I-I didn't want him to hurt you Mama."

"You let me handle my business! You hear?!"

"Y-yes Mama." Lamar turned and ran into his room crying. Mama looked down the hall and turned towards my bedroom door. Her face was all bloody and swollen. Blood was running down her nose and she wiped it off with the back of her hand. My heart started pounding again as I watched her stare at my door. Finally, she turned and walked into her bedroom. I eased the door shut and walked towards my bed. All of a sudden my bedroom door burst open. Splinters flew in every direction as Mama bolted into my room huffing and puffing;

"You ain't nothing but trouble for me Gina. Ever since the day you was born. I'm tired of your mess!"

I didn't know whether to speak or be quiet. I just stood by the side of the bed watching and waiting for her to move or say something.

"You done caused me to lose the best man I ever had. What you got to say for yo' self?"

"Mama, I didn't mean to come out there yelling. I'm sorry."

"You sorry?! Sorry won't bring Carl back."

Mama charged over to where I was and that's when I saw the belt in her hands. She started whipping me with all her might. I felt the belt as it hit my arms and then my legs. A couple of times the belt landed across my back as I was trying to turn to protect myself from the blows of the belt. She pushed me down and instead of falling on the bed, I slid down the side onto the floor. Mama started kicking me. I curled my body into a ball hoping she would stop before I ended up in the hospital again. The last kick caught me in the stomach and I screamed. The sound of the scream must have brought her back to her senses or maybe it was Lamar's crying and begging her to stop. Mama looked down at me and turned and left the room without saying a word. I stayed on the floor. My stomach was hurting so bad, I couldn't move and I was gasping for breath.

"Gina, you ok?"

"Leave me alone Lamar." I whispered. Although he probably saved my life, I didn't want his pity. Most of the whippings that I'd had in life were because of him. I still blamed him for a lot of Mama's meanness towards me. I was finally able to pull myself up off of the floor and it wasn't until then that I realized that I had wet myself. It must have happened when Mama kicked me in the stomach. I hobbled to my dresser and got some clean underwear and a nightgown. I slowly opened my door and crept to the bathroom and got myself cleaned up. I sat on the toilet for several minutes until the pain in my stomach subsided enough for me to stand up. After the pain in my stomach died down, I noticed my head was pounding like crazy. I thought I was going to pass out. How could Mama attack me like she did knowing that I had just come out of the hospital? She could have hit me in the head and broke my stitches. I wanted to die. As I was coming out of the bathroom, I heard Mama in the living room crying like a baby.

"Gina? Come here baby."

I knew what was coming. It was that same old apology that meant nothing. I crept down the hall holding my stomach. My whole body had begun to feel sore and all I wanted to do was go to bed. I leaned against the wall as I stood at the end of the hallway looking at Mama sitting in the chair by the front door. She was rocking back and forth with tears and snot running down her face.

"Yes, Mama." I said as I stood watching her. She disgusted me and I didn't want to be anywhere near her.

"Come here baby." She said as she continued to rock back and forth. I didn't want her to touch me, but I didn't want to make her snap again. So I slowly made my way over to stand beside her chair.

She looked up at me still crying. "Gina, Mama sorry. I don't know what came over me. I get so mad sometimes. When Carl walked out, I lost it. Forgive Mama, ok?" She reached out and wrapped her arm around me. I squinted as a wave a pain shot through my stomach. She was squeezing me too tightly. I bit my lip as the pain shot through my body.

"I forgive you Mama." I said and laid an arm around her shoulder. As much as I hated her at that moment, I also felt sorry for her. I felt sorry because she had no clue about being a mother or loving someone.

"Thank you baby."

"Mama, is it ok if I go to bed?" I asked softly. I was afraid that she would jump up and slap me.

"Yeah baby, you go on to bed. Nite nite."

"Good night Mama." I managed to drag myself back down the hall to my bedroom. Lamar was sitting in his room looking at me as I passed by.

"Lamar, I'm sorry for being mean when you were trying to help me. Thanks for trying to help."

"You welcome Gina."

I walked into my room and closed the door. I turned the lock and realized that it didn't matter because that part of the door had been broken when Mama came into my room. I didn't bother trying to put the dresser behind it because Mr. Carl wouldn't be spending the night. I turned my little night light on and slowly slid under the covers. I opened my nightstand drawer and looked at the bottle of painkillers the doctor had given me. I looked at the little brown bottle with the white cap and I thought about my life again. I looked at what had happened over the past week. The rape was nothing compared to what had happened the past week with Mama. There was no biological connection with Mr. Carl, but Mama was different. She was the woman who had carried me for nine months and had given me life. Now, she was doing everything she could to destroy that same life. I felt like the umbilical cord had been cut before I was born and all ties to her had been severed. I was dying slowly every day and there was no life support system for me. I didn't understand how she could hate me the way that she did. The tears flowed as I lay there looking at the pills. I picked up the bottle and took the cap off. I poured out about ten of the pills in my hand. I wanted to die and not feel the pain anymore. I wanted to escape the loneliness. I was ready to let go.

I am not sure what made me look back into the drawer, but I did. That's when I saw my little green bible that someone had given me. I laid the pills on the table and picked up the bible. I flipped it open and saw the twenty third Psalms and began to read. I read that chapter over and over until the tears flowed freely. I remembered how my grandparents had always talked about the faith of a mustard seed and how just a little bit of faith can bring you through your troubles. I realized that I had let go of my faith in God. I didn't have the answers to my questions as to why things turned out the way that they did, but at the same time I had stopped believing that God could bring me through. I believed that God was real. I believed that he could do the impossible because my grandparents had told me how he did things for them. I put the pills back in the bottle and I told myself that I wanted to live. I was going to finish school and leave Mama's house and never look back. I prayed for God to give me the strength to do just that. As I lay my head on the pillow, I actually smiled in spite of the tears that were rolling down my cheek. For the first time in my young life, I had set a goal for myself. A goal that I believed I would one day accomplish.

Chapter 11
When It Rains It Pours

I thought I was at the lowest point in my life and nothing could be worse than the sexual abuse I had already suffered at the hands of Mr. Carl. I was wrong. Two weeks had passed since the night I thought about committing suicide. On Sunday evening about six o'clock the phone rang and Mama answered it. I was sitting outside on the porch talking to Lamar about a video game we wanted when I heard Mama screaming. We both ran into the house to see what was wrong.

"Mama! What's wrong?!" Lamar and I said at the same time.

Mama was lying on the floor crying like a baby with the phone clutched in her hands. We knelt down beside her. I pried the phone out of her hand and listened to see if anyone was still on there.

"Hello?"

"Gina, is that you?"

"Cousin Marion? What's wrong? Are you crying?"

"Gina, something terrible has happened," she said as her voice broke and I could hear her sobbing. Oh God, I thought. What now? My heart began pounding in my chest and I felt sick. Cousin Marion rarely called us, if ever. Even though she lived next door to my grandparents and was close to them, she and Mama never got along because of a silly dispute over a boy when they were teenagers.

"Gina, it's about Papa & Mimi?" Those were the names that she called my grandparents. I felt something wet sliding down my face and realized I was crying. My head began to pound as fast as my heart was beating and I knew right then that something was terribly wrong. Cousin Marion couldn't talk for crying so hard.

I waited for Cousin Marion to keep talking, but there was a moment of silence. Then I heard another voice on the phone. It was Jake, Cousin Marion's husband. "Gina, this is Jake. I got some bad news. Your grandparents had a head-on collision with an eighteen wheeler on the way home from church today. Child, they didn't make it. I'm sorry." Jake's voice broke too at the end as he broke down in tears.

I dropped the phone and Lamar looked at my face in anticipation of learning what was happening. "Grandma and Granddaddy are gone Lamar," I whispered. He frowned at me trying to register in his mind what I was saying.

"They're dead."

"Dead?" Gina, that ain't funny." He said. Lamar was looking at me and waiting to see me crack a smile.

"You know I wouldn't joke about something like that Lamar." I said as the tears flowed.

"Dead?"

He began to cry as he whispered that one single word. For the first time in our lives, the three of us, Mama, Lamar, and me sat together hugging as we cried over our loss. My grandparents meant everything to me and going to visit them was the one bright spot in my world of darkness. I went through a range of emotions as I thought about life without them. I was hurting because I wouldn't ever see them again or speak to them, but I was angry because they were leaving me alone. A part of me wished that I would have been with them. I would have been able to escape the pain in my own life. On the other hand, I felt a little peace because I knew that they were going to a better place and that I would see them again one day in heaven.

I'm not sure how long the three of us sat on the floor, but by the time Mama got up and moved to her bed, the room was slightly dark. No one said anything. I helped Lamar up and we walked down the hallway side-by-side and went to our rooms. I laid down on my bed and cried some more. My body felt weak and I was thankful to feel a wave of sleepiness wash over me. I welcomed its soothing effect because I didn't want to think or remember at that moment.

The next morning the sun shining through the pale yellow curtains woke me up. Sometime during the night I had haphazardly pulled the covers over me, but I was still in the same clothes that I had worn the day before. I sat up on the edge of the bed and let my feet hang over the side. My head was hurting and my eyes felt slightly swollen. It was still hard to believe that yesterday had been real. My grandparents were gone. No more fun summers or great cooking or fishing trips. I remembered the way would sit on their front porch in the evenings after dinner and granddaddy would tell one of his funny stories about something that happened when he was younger. My grandmother would chime in and make it even funnier by adding something granddaddy had forgotten. Even though Lamar and I had heard those stories over and over, we never got tired of hearing them because each time something else was added that was different from the last time.

"Gina?"

I looked up and saw Lamar standing in my doorway. His eyes were as red as a cherry and swollen. Seeing him made me cry.

"Yeah?"

"Is it really true? Was yesterday for real?"

"Yeah. I know. I asked myself the same thing. Where's Mama?"

"She in her room. Hadn't been out all morning. Should we knock on the door?"

"No. We shouldn't bother her."

"Ok. I'm going back to my room." He turned and shuffled back across the hall to his room.

It was around noon before Mama finally came out of her room. Lamar and I had dressed and cleaned our rooms. We were watching tv in the living room.

"How you feelin' Mama?" Lamar asked as she came into the room and sat down.

"My head hurts. Anybody call?"

"No ma'am."

"Mama, you want something to eat or drink?" I asked.

"No. You can bring me a glass of water and a Goody powder for this headache."

I quickly walked into the kitchen and fixed the water and found the box of Goody powder. Mama took it without saying a word. Somebody finally called and I heard Mama saying that the family had to make funeral arrangements and call everybody. It was a quiet day in our house and each of us dealt with the loss of my grandparents.

Chapter 12
The Funeral

It had been a week since that fatal accident that took my grandparents away. Mama and Cousin Marion had worked together to contact as many relatives as possible. On the day of the funeral Mama, Lamar and me got up early and got dressed. Mama wore a simple black two piece suit. Lamar wore a pair of black slacks and a long sleeved white dress shirt. I had on a long black dress that Cousin Marion had bought for me because I didn't have anything else to wear. Cousin Marion picked us up and drove us to my grandparents' house. As we pulled up into the driveway, I was amazed at all of the people that were standing around outside talking. I saw aunts, uncles, and cousins that I hadn't seen in a long time. Some people were laughing and others were teary-eyed. We got out of the car and walked up the walkway.

"Hey Bertha, baby. How are you holding up child?" Aunt Ella asked. She was grandaddy's oldest sister. She looked stylish in her long black skirt and matching jacket. She wore a black hat with a wide brim that came down low over her eyes. Aunt Ella was around seventy years old, but she still moved around like she was twenty years younger. She was tall, thin, and still had very good posture. A few curls of her gray hair peaked from under the brim of her hat in the back. Aunt Ella had dark eyes that almost looked black and she had almost perfect eyesight because she had laser surgery a few years ago. She had a piercing look and when she looked at me sometimes I felt she could see straight to my soul. She was a sweet woman and I wished

I could have spent more time around her, but she lived in South Carolina and didn't get a chance to visit often. Aunt Ella was Cousin Marion's mom.

"I'm alright Auntie. How you?" Mama mumbled as Auntie Ella hugged her. I saw Mama tense her body as Aunt Ella embraced her. For a second I thought she wouldn't return the hug, but finally her arms wrapped around Aunt Ella's thin frame for a brief hug. Aunt Ella stepped back and looked at Mama.

"I'm making it by the help of the good Lord child. I'm gonna miss my brother and sister-in-law." Her voice broke at the end and tears rolled down her cheeks.

Mama let a sob and rushed passed her into the house. Lamar and I followed close behind. There were more people gathered in the house sitting down and talking. Mama had found a seat in the corner of the living room and sat down wiping her eyes. We didn't wait long before the police escort and the limo arrived. Everybody went outside to prepare for the car line up. My grandparents' pastor, Rev. Leonard, had arrived and was gathering everybody in a circle to pray. We got to ride in the first limo with Mama, Aunt Ella, and Cousin Marion since we all were the closest family. The ride to the church seemed like it took forever even though it was only three blocks away. The funeral home director got out of the car and opened the doors. We all got out and again followed directions to line up before going into the church.

Cousin Marion had convinced Mama to let the caskets stay open for out-of-town relatives to view the bodies before the funeral service began. I was kind of glad that she did because Mama had refused to go the funeral home to see them after the accident. I was angry with her for that because I had wanted to tell my grandparents good-bye. So today I would be able to see them and whisper my good-byes.

The sound of Mama's voice brought me out of my thoughts. "No! I will not go in that church long as them caskets open Marion!"

"Bertha, calm down. Please, don't make a scene today of all days. You should want to see your parents one last time."

Cousin Marion was patting Mama on the back and trying to console her, but Mama shrugged her hand away. Aunt Ella came up and pulled Mama aside. By that time Mama was crying and the tears were streaming down her face. I felt sorry for her because I knew a part of the reason that she couldn't stand the idea of seeing them in the casket. It was because of how horribly she had treated them when they were living. Although my grandmother hadn't been the best mother in the world, she had tried at times to talk to Mama and develop a better relationship. Mama wouldn't listen and had pretty much isolated herself from talking to them on the phone or visiting. I was glad that she didn't keep Lamar and me from our grandparents or that would have been devastating.

"L-l-l-isten Auntie, I don't want to see them lying there in them caskets. Please, don't make me do it!" Mama cried.

I had walked over a little closer so I could hear what Aunt Ella was saying and had caught the last part of their conversation. "Ok. Look, here is what we will do. After everyone has viewed the body, then I will come back out and get you and we can walk in together and sit with the family. Ok?" Aunt Ella said in a soothing voice.

"Alright. Thanks, Auntie. At least somebody understand how I feel. " Mama sniffed and rolled her eyes at Cousin Marion who pretended not to notice.

Mama, backing down? Now that was a new one, but maybe she had too much sorrow and pain right now to deal with anything else. She stepped to the side as the rest of us lined up. The mortician led the way, followed by the minister, and the family began walking in. There were so many people, black and white, already seated and I recognized a lot of the faces from my grandparents' neighborhood. Some faces I didn't recognize.

Lamar and me were behind Cousin Marion. Ahead of us, I saw the two caskets lined up next to each other. They were both black and shiny. Each one had a large flower arrangement on top of it. Some of the flowers were white and yellow roses and I am not sure about the others because I never remember the names of flowers. Aunt Ella walked up first to my grandmother and then to my granddaddy. I heard her sobbing and it was soft compared to the way her shoulders were shaking. As she stood at my granddaddy's casket, she swayed and Cousin Jake and a couple of the other men caught her and helped her to a nearby pew.

The line slowly moved up and before I knew it Lamar and me were next. We had been holding hands the hold time and as we got ready to move up, Lamar squeezed my hand so hard that I would have screamed out in any other situation. I gently squeezed his back to let him know that I wouldn't let go as we walked up to the caskets. We looked at my grandmother first. She looked like she was sleeping as she lay there in her white dress with the lace collar. She was wearing white gloves. They had even put on her favorite rose colored lipstick. She didn't look dead at all. I touched her cheek and that's when the tears flowed. She was so cold and her skin felt more like leather than flesh. She was really gone. I started to shake, but I was determined to say my good-byes. I leaned over to her ear and whispered, "I'll never forget you and what you taught me. I love you grandma. There's so many things that I needed to tell. I'm going to miss you so much. Good-bye."

Lamar stood beside me crying. I put my arm around him and moved over to granddaddy's casket. He was wearing a black suit with a white shirt and black tie. I touch his cheek and felt the same coldness that I had felt with my grandma. I stared at granddaddy's face as hard as I could because I never wanted to forget his face. I leaned over and whispered the same words to him. I touched his cold cheek one last time before Lamar and me walked over to the family pews and sat beside Cousin Marion.

After everyone had viewed the bodies, they closed the caskets. Aunt Ella was too distraught to go back outside and get Mama, so she sent Cousin Jake to do it. The rest of the service went by in a blur. I don't remember much of what the preacher said because I sat there the hold time thinking of all the fun times that I had shared with my grandparents. Mama had come in and sat between Lamar and Cousin Marion. She cried the whole time. I couldn't hear what the preacher was saying because of all of the crying. After he finished his message, we all got up to line up again and get in the limo to ride to the cemetery. Cars parked behind each other in a single line and walked to the big tent where chairs had been set out. The funeral home director gave each of us a white rose. I thought viewing the bodies was hard, but watching them lower the caskets into the ground was worse. It was final. They were gone forever. We all walked up and threw the white roses into the grave. I watched as some of them fell on the casket while others fell to the ground. By the time we left, everyone was in tears. The ride back home was long and silent.

Chapter 13
Moving Forward

It has been three months since the funeral. I still miss my grandparents and I still cry whenever I think about our time together. My granddaddy left the house to Mama. She said that she'd move back there, but not right away. It was still too painful to walk in there knowing that they weren't there. Lamar became distant and withdrawn as he dealt with his own pain. I became more determined than ever to get myself ready to leave home after high school.

My last two years of high school flew by rather quickly. During that time I was able to focus on my grades and became an "A" student again. I went to see the guidance counselor and learned everything I could about preparing for college and applying for student loans. Any chances of getting a scholarship had been blown because of the low grades I got during my freshman and sophomore years of high school. I took as many college prep classes as I could squeeze into my schedule. I took the SAT and scored quite high on it. My score was high enough to get me accepted at one of the major universities in the South. By end of my senior year I was very excited. I chose a large school because I wanted to be a face in the crowd. I didn't want to have to worry about too much attention from people and making friends. I had no trust in people and I planned to keep to myself.

The day of graduation finally came. As I went to stand in line I found Lamar and Mama in the crowd. Mama was all emotional and Lamar seemed quite sad. He and I had finally grown close after he got past losing our grandparents and after he learned what Mama had let

Mr. Carl do to me. He was growing up. At fourteen years old he was already six feet tall. As I looked at him I prayed that he would finish high school and leave like I was going to do. He was very smart and athletic. I figured he would end up getting a scholarship to some school for basketball. The line started moving and Mama and Lamar went to find a good seat. Thank you Lord! It was finally here! I was graduating from high school! I would still have to spend the summer at home because college classes didn't start until August. I decided to spend the three months working and I had been offered a job at the local supermarket. The pay wasn't great, but at least I would have some money to start me off.

"Gina Jones," called Mr. Moreman, our high school principal.

I got up and quickly walked up to the stage to get my diploma. I had been so absorbed in my thoughts that I had missed hearing the keynote speaker and most of my classmates getting their degree. When I walked across the stage Lamar and Mama were waving and cheering. I smiled, shook Mr. Moreman's hand, and accepted my diploma. As I was walking back to my seat, I remembered something my granddaddy always told me and that was if you get an education, get something in your head, and then nobody could take that away from you. I raised my diploma in the air as I silently saluted my grandparents who I felt were watching from above and smiling down on me. The last name was finally called and Mr. Moreman told us all to stand and turn our tassels. He congratulated us for our victory of finishing high school and at the end we all shouted with joy and threw our caps into the air. Lamar was the first one to run up to me and give me a hug while Mama stood back and watched. She managed to smile at me and told me that she was proud of me. Most of the graduates had made plans to meet at one of the few local hangouts in town, the bowling alley, after graduation. Out of courtesy, one of the girls asked me if I wanted to come, but I declined. I had never really been a part of their circle and I felt no need to try now and become involved. Besides, I wouldn't have known what to say or how to act. So I followed Mama and Lamar to the red 1985 Ford Taurus that belonged to my Grandma. I liked that car except for the color. Red cars stood out and attracted too much attention, especially from the cops. One day I was going to have a nice sporty car and it would be a color that was not very noticeable.

The summer flew by like I knew it would and the day came for me to leave home. Lamar was happy for me although he kept saying that he was really going to miss me. Mama didn't say she would miss me, but she had mentioned several times that she wished I would change my mind and find a job at home to help her out with the bills. I figured she had truly lost her mind if she believed I would stay in her house another day. I was thankful that she drove me to college and she wouldn't have if I didn't agree to give her money for gas and pay for the overnight hotel fee.

It took us about seven hours to get there. I had gotten my license over the summer. Mama had taught Lamar and me to drive four years ago and I was a really good driver, but I couldn't drive anywhere until I got my license. I was excited about finally leaving for college and even more so when Mama let me drive the entire trip. I had to keep reminding myself not to speed in my excitement to get there. Mama and Lamar slept most of the way which worked well for me. I didn't have to worry about meaningless small talk or complaining from Mama. I could see the signs for the university just ahead and had to go one more mile before turning off of the expressway. Mama and Lamar woke up about the same time.

"Gina, slow down."

"Yes ma'am."

"Where we at?" asked Lamar.

"Almost there. The school is about two more miles away." I said smiling.

"Hmmph. That didn't take long as I thought." Mama said as she struggled to get comfortable in her seat. She had gained more weight in the past two years since Mr. Carl had left and I believed she was easily pushing three hundred pounds.

We entered the campus of the university and I glanced around at all of the huge buildings. Most of them looked like they were new. The grass was green and there were lots and lots of flowers and shrubs. It was so beautiful. One of the things I liked about the school already was that they had signs and maps to show where all the buildings were located. I followed the directions to get to the dorm that I was living in. Actually, it was more like an apartment than a dorm. The brochure they had sent me showed pictures of the apartments. Each one had four bedrooms with separate bathrooms, a living room, a dining room, and a kitchen. I had never seen anything as nice as those apartments. I pulled up to the apartment building that had been assigned in the letter the university sent me along with my acceptance letter.

"Mmm…these nice here."

I got out and walked up to the door and it opened just as I reached the little doormat that was lying in front of it. A white lady with dark brown hair was standing there smiling. She looked to be in her forties.

"Hi there. You must be Gina?"

"Yes ma'am. I am."

"Welcome to Boxley University. My name is Ginny Vinson and I am the dorm mother for all the girls who live in The Palms Apartments."

"Nice to meet you Ms. Vinson." Lamar and Mama had come up behind me as Ms. Vinson was introducing herself. "Ms. Vinson, this is my mother Bertha Jones and my brother Lamar."

"Hi Ms. Jones, Lamar."

"Hi, nice to meet you," Mama said.

"Hi." Lamar said as he shuffled from one foot to the other.

"Well, come on in you all. I can show you around the apartment. Gina, your roommates haven't arrived yet so you'll get to meet them later."

As we walked into the apartment I had to keep myself from acting like I'd never seen nice things. The apartment was more beautiful than the pictures in the brochure. As soon as we stepped into the door, I saw the living room on the right. It was furnished with two big sofas and two big chairs. I had never seen furniture quite like it. I liked the burgundy and gold colors that were in the fabric. The walls were all painted ivory. Ms. Vinson was talking about the huge TV that was sitting on an entertainment system. I learned that all of the apartments had cable connections in the living room and all of the bedrooms. She said that if I had a TV that I could connect to the cable in my bedroom too. I didn't have a TV and had no idea when I would be able to afford one. Besides, I didn't need any distractions because I planned on spending most of my study time in my bedroom. On the left of the doorway was the kitchen and the dining room area. It was just as nice as the living room. There was a nice wooden table and chair set in the dining room and the kitchen was kind of small, but nicely equipped. In front of us were some stairs and Ms. Vinson was leading Lamar and Mama up them towards the bedrooms. I quickly followed. She told us that all of the bedrooms were identical and told me that I could choose any one of them I wanted. At the top of the stairs was a little hallway that went two ways and with two bedrooms on each side. I chose the last bedroom on the left side because it was on the side of the kitchen and I figured it would be quieter than the two bedrooms over the living room. Ms. Vinson opened the door and told me to come and see what the room looked like. I walked to where she was standing and looked in. I was totally amazed at the size of the room. The brochure didn't show the whole room, just the bed and desk. There was a nice twin bed with a headboard against one wall, a dresser with a mirror in front of it, and a desk with a few bookshelves. The room had a big window with heavy beige curtains draped over it. The bathroom had a sink, toilet, and a shower. I was going to love spending time here I thought to myself. Lamar told me that he really liked the room and wished he had one like it back home. Mama didn't say a word.

Ms. Vinson gave me my keys to the apartment and to my bedroom. She gave me her apartment number and contact information as she was leaving. I thanked her and we all went outside. Lamar and I started getting my stuff out of the car while Mama went back in and sat down in the living room. It took us only a few minutes to unpack the car and carry everything up to my room. Finally, we were done and went to join Mama in the living room.

"Man, Gina, this place is da bomb!"

"Yeah, I had no idea it would be this nice. You like it Mama?"

"It don't make no difference whether I like it or not. I ain't the one who gonna be living here." Mama said as she stood up from the sofa. "You gonna show me how to get to that hotel. My head hurt and I want to take a nap."

"You don't want to see the campus Mama?" I asked hoping she would at least act like she was interested in the place where I would be spending my next four years.

"Didn't I say my head hurt?"

"Mama, I'm hungry." Lamar said as he stood up and followed Mama who was now halfway to the door.

"Well, yo' sistah can take you to get something to eat after she drop me off at the hotel. I ain't feelin' too good."

Good, I thought to myself. I could keep the car for a couple hours and drive around and get to see what the city of Boxley looked like and see the campus. We all walked out of the apartment and I locked the door behind us. My belongings were locked up safely in my bedroom. It didn't take long to find the hotel where Mama and Lamar would be spending the night. I got them checked in and gave Mama one of the key cards. She told us not to worry about her and to take our time in coming back. I don't know what changed her mood, but it was working for me. We promised to bring her back something to eat as she went into the room and shut the door.

Lamar and I drove around for almost two hours as we learned more about the city and the school. Boxley had a population over thirty thousand people. It was a pretty decent sized place and had a little shopping mall on the outskirts of town. The university had a little over five thousand students in which about half of them were local residents. There were local hangouts for the college students: two bowling alleys, a skating rink, and two movie theaters. On campus, there was a recreational building that had a café, a movie theatre, and a gymnasium. I found out that we had full access to the gym which offered all types of exercise classes and we could even take swimming lessons in the pool. I was excited about that because I had always wanted to learn how to swim. After our sightseeing even Lamar was excited and told me that he was going to come to school at Boxley when he graduated from high school. I was proud to hear him say that, because I feared that Mama would find a way to keep him at home with her. Lamar was a smart boy and had begun to make really good grades. He loved sports and his favorite one was basketball. As a high school freshman he was already starting to get letters from several colleges. Boxley had a good basketball team, but it wasn't known as one of the top schools for its sports. Nonetheless, I am sure that Lamar could still get a scholarship if he chose to attend there.

"Hey Gina."

"Yeah Lamar."

"I'm gonna miss you."

"Yeah right."

"No, for real. I know I ain't been the best brother. 'Specially when I was little, but I changed. I think you are a great big sis." He was smiling sheepishly as he told me this.

I glanced at him as I kept on driving towards the hotel. "Thanks Lamar. You alright too. You and I have been getting along well the past couple of years, so I don't hold anything against you."

"Gina, how is it that you manage to speak so proper. I mean, for as long as I can remember, you never sounded like us."

"I guess I never thought about that much. In school the teachers are always on us by telling us to pronounce this word correctly, use this verb and not that one, and all that. So, it must have rubbed off on me without my noticing it."

"They tell us too, but I don't pay much attention to that. All the fellas think it's cool to speak like me."

"See, that's the problem. You trying to fit in with the fellas," I teased.

"I don't try to, but I like hanging out. I wish you'd had made friends."

"We're different Lamar. I just feel more comfortable by myself."

"Yeah, I know why. All that stuff with Mama and—"

"Don't!" I snapped. Today was a happy one for me and I didn't want to spend time bringing up painful memories.

"What?"

"Let's change the subject. Today is a happy one for me. Let's not bring up things that don't really matter right now."

"I'm sorry. I wasn't trying to bring you down or nothing." Lamar said dropping his head. I knew that his feelings were hurt and that he wasn't trying to be mean to me in what he had been saying.

"I know. Hey, I'm sorry too. I shouldn't have snapped at you. I know you didn't mean any harm little brother."

We pulled up into the parking lot of the hotel. It was just getting dark and I could see the light on in Mama's room. Since I had a key card I used it to open the door. Mama was sitting on the bed watching TV.

"You feelin' better Mama?" asked Lamar.

"Yeah, that old headache eased up a bit."

"Here's the food we promised to bring back Mama." I said as I handed her the box. I had stopped at a little restaurant near the hotel and bought her chicken, mashed potatoes, peas, and a dinner roll. She mumbled thanks, took the box, and set it beside the bed on the nightstand.

"Mama, do you feel like taking me back to campus?"

"Naw, I ain't feelin' like driving. You can take the car tonight and come back early in the mornin'. I want to leave around nine. So you gonna need to be here at eight and I'll take you back."

"Ok. I'll make sure that the car is full of gas before I come back."

I tried to control my excitement as I said goodnight and walked out of the hotel room.

I decided that I wanted to get settled in at the apartment and unpack my things. As I pulled up to my apartment building, I saw that the lights were on in the living room. One of my roommates must have arrived because I did not leave any of the lights on. I hadn't thought about the fact that it would probably be dark by the time I got back from the hotel. I got of the car, locking the door behind me, and walked up to the door. It opened just as I was about to put the key in the lock. A tall, dark-skinned girl opened the door. She was about an inch or so taller than me with long, black hair pulled back into a ponytail. She was wearing a white t-shirt with the word "princess" written in pink letters across the chest and a pair of faded blue jean shorts.

"Hi! Come in. I saw your headlights as you pulled up. You must be Gina."

"Hi, yes I am." I said as she stepped aside to let me in. "What's your name?"

"I am Celeste Simmons. I got here about an hour ago."

"Nice to meet you Celeste. Have any of the other roommates arrived?"

"Nah, not yet. They might not get in until tomorrow."

"Oh ok." I said after a few minutes of silence. I always hated that brief period of silence when nobody knew what to say. I had never been one to talk a lot, especially with people I didn't know well.

"Hey, since we are the only two here, you want to go get something to eat?"

"Uhhhmm. I ate already. My mom and brother drove up with me. They are at a hotel for the night and we grabbed a bite to eat before I came back here."

"Oh ok. I think I'll walk over to the café on campus and grab a sandwich. You're welcome to come."

All I wanted to do was go up to my room, unpack and enjoy the peace and quiet of having a place without Mama. On the other hand, I didn't want Celeste to think that I was rude or unfriendly.

"Ok, sure."

It took us about five minutes to walk over to the café. As we entered, I noticed that there were about five other kids sitting at tables chatting. The café was really nice. It wasn't very large, but not small either. As I glanced around, I estimated that about eighty to a hundred people could easily fit into the sitting area. There were nice square tables set up at one end for eating. At the other end, there was a nice sized television and several plush, brown leather sofas and chairs organized so that you could see the television no matter where you were sitting. Celeste and I walked over to the counter for her to place her order. She asked if I wanted anything, but I declined. I had brought all the money that I had saved over the summer and figured that if I watched my spending, then I may be able to get it to last for at least four months.

"So, Gina, where are you from again?"

"I am from a little town about 7 hours away called Pikesville."

"Oh, I've never heard of that. I'm from upstate New York. This is my second year at Boxley and I am still trying to get used to the summer heat."

I smiled as she laughed and kept telling me more about herself. I learned that Celeste was majoring in chemistry and she had her dreams set on being a top research scientist. She had come to Boxley on a basketball scholarship which was paying for the entire four years of college. I wondered if she knew how blessed she was by having that scholarship. I had ended up applying for a student loan for the first year and hopefully, I would be able to find a job by my sophomore year to help cover most of my expenses so that my loans would be small.

"Do you play any sports?"

"Huh?"

"Girl, were you daydreaming on me?"

"I'm sorry Celeste. I didn't mean to be rude. I am a little tired after the long drive that I had today to get here."

"Gina, I am the one who should apologize. I have been rattling on and on about myself and I should have thought about the fact that you might be tired. Come on, let's go back to the apartment."

We got back to the apartment and I told Celeste that I was going to call it a night because I had to get up early the next morning and take the car back to Mama. I climbed the stairs and walked down the hall to my room door. I smiled as I put the little key into the lock and opened the door. I quietly shut it behind me and locked it. I started to unpack the few things that I had brought from home and after about an hour I had completely organized my bedroom. I had a poster of horses on the wall facing the bed. It had been given to me one year by my granddaddy. On my dresser I had put a blue, glass figurine of a dolphin and a snow globe with a little brown and yellow cottage inside. These were things that had once belonged to my grandma and I remembered playing with those as a child whenever we were at her house. I hung my clothes in the closet and neatly stacked my shoes on the floor underneath. I thanked God for allowing me to get that job at the store over the summer. I had been able to save some money and use the other part to buy some new clothes and shoes to start off the school year. I looked down at the four pairs of shoes and realized that I had never in my life had more than two pairs of shoes at a time. The clothes still had the store tags hanging on them and I would remove each one as I wore that particular outfit. I looked at the bed and admired the white bedspread that Mama had given me. It must have been at least fifteen years old, but it stilled looked new. Mama always took good care of all of her stuff. The spread had rose petal designs in it and the edges hung down in frills. At the foot of the bed was a burgundy and white quilt that my grandma had made for me three Christmases ago. The quilt was heavy, but it was soft and warm. I loved to curl up in it and read a book during the winter time.

I set the alarm clock that I'd bought with some of my savings, got out my sleeping shirt, and took a shower. The warm water felt good against my skin as I stood there marveling in the fact that it was my bathroom. The walls were colored the same ivory color as the rest of the apartment. The shower was enclosed with a frosted shower door. I decided that I would get some things to decorate the bathroom as soon as I could get to the shopping center. Finally, I stepped out of the bathroom and slid beneath the crisp, clean sheets on my bed. I reached over and turned off the little lamp on the night table.

Chapter 14
The Last Straw

Three months have flown by rather quickly as I realize that my first semester is drawing to an end. In a couple of weeks it will be Thanksgiving and I will have almost a week off before we come back for two more weeks of course work and final exams. Lamar and I talked at least two to three times a week. Sometimes Mama would say a brief hello or ask me how I was doing but we never talked longer than a couple of minutes. It was the week before Thanksgiving and Lamar called just as I was getting ready to go to bed.

"Hello?"

"Gina, it's Lamar."

"What's up bro'? Isn't it past your bedtime?"

"Yeah, but I wanted to talk to my big sis."

"Everything ok?"

"Yeah, it's all good. I just wanted to know if you gave it any mo' thought."

"What?"

"You know. Next week."

"Ohhh. You don't give up do you?" I said smiling as I admired my little brother's persistence to get me to come home for Thanksgiving.

"Gina, I miss you for real. Besides, it actually feels like we are closer now than when you were here. It'd be good to have you home for a few days."

"I know. I agree. I'll come home. You have no idea about the sacrifice I am making for you."

"Yeah I do. I really do."

"Cool. I'll see you next week. I can catch the bus all the way to Pikesville. Will Mama pick me up?"

"Yeah, she said she would. I'll be there too."

"Ok. Now let me get some sleep."

"A'ight. See you next week."

I put the phone down and lay in the bed looking up at the ceiling. I really didn't want to go home. I had already gotten permission from Ms. Vinson to stay in the apartment over the break because she wouldn't be leaving for Thanksgiving, but would be gone for Christmas. Lamar had sounded so disappointed when I told him that I wouldn't be coming home and he had been pleading with me to change my mind for the last couple of days. Mama had said nothing whenever I called home and I figured she didn't care one way or another. I really didn't want to have to put up with any of her negativity during the holidays, but I didn't want Lamar to have to be alone at home with her.

A week passed by all too soon and before I knew it I was sitting on the Greyhound bus heading for Pikesville two days before Thanksgiving. The only thing I hated about riding the bus was the fact that there were two forty five minute layovers before I got home. I had bought a mystery novel to read for the long trip home which ended up being over nine hours. It was dark by the time the bus pulled up into the station and I could see Lamar and Mama standing outside waiting. Lamar ran up to me and gave me the biggest bear hug as I stepped down off of the bus.

"Hey Sis! 'Bout time you got here." Lamar had a big grin on his face as he gave me another big bear hug.

"Yeah, tell me about it. That was a long ride. Easy on the hug there, I've only been gone three months not three years." I laughed as I wiggled out of his hug.

"No doubt. My bad, I missed ya. Hey, I'll get your bags. Mama is over there waiting. Go and say somethin' to her."

"What are you now? A go-between?" I said as I looked over to where Mama was standing beside the car. She was smoking a cigarette. She didn't even look my way.

"Nahh," he said laughing, "I just want us all to have a good Thanksgiving."

I walked over to where Mama was standing puffing on a cigarette. "Hey Mama."

"Hey. What took you so long to get here?"

"The bus had a flat tire. I'm sorry you had to wait."

"Hmmph. Guess it wasn't yo' fault."

"How you doing?"

"I'm fine." She snapped. "Lamar come on here and put them bags in the car. I'm ready to go." Mama yelled to Lamar as she wobbled to the car.

Mama had really picked up weight. She was even larger than she had been when I'd last seen her. I don't remember ever seeing her as big as she was now. I wondered why she was gaining so much weight. Lamar had grown another inch and I figured he was going to look like a giant by the time he reached eighteen. He brought my luggage to the car and loaded it into the trunk before jumping into the passenger side as Mama started the engine. It took about ten minutes to get from the bus station to the apartment. Mama still hadn't moved back into my grandparents' house. I couldn't understand why she would struggle to keep paying rent when she had a house that was already paid for. The apartment still looked the same as we pulled up to the curb and parked. I helped get my stuff out of the trunk as Mama went on ahead and unlocked the door. Nothing had changed on the inside either and my room still looked like it did the day I left it.

"Gina, Mama keeps your room clean and everything like she expecting you to come back or something." Lamar whispered as he brought my big suitcase into the room and set it beside the bed.

"Yeah right."

"I'm for real. I think she thought you wouldn't like college and come back home."

"Lamar, let me tell you something. I only came back for your sake this time. There is nothing here for me besides you. There are too many bad memories here and I'd rather just stay away. Besides, Mama acts like I'm some stranger. We don't have any kind of relationship. Hadn't you noticed?

"Yeah, I noticed. I know this hard for you. I 'preciate your coming home Gina. I want to be just like you one day when I finish school. I'm leaving too."

"For real?"

"Yeah. Don't sound so shocked. My b-ball coach thinks I got a good chance of getting a scholarship. So in three more years I'll be out of here."

"Lamar, I've prayed that you would grow up and do something positive with your life. I'm happy to hear that you have plans."

"You pray about everythang don't ya?"

"Pretty much."

"You know all the kids always thought you were too religious."

"What?!"

"Yeah They did."

I laughed as I thought how surprising it was to hear that bit of news. I never thought anyone at school paid me any attention. Lamar and I talked for a long while and we laughed as we shared stories about things that had happened in our lives over the past three months. I could hear Mama shuffling around in the kitchen as Lamar left to go to his room. I decided that I would take the initiative and be the one to break the ice. I walked down the hallway to the kitchen and found Mama sitting at the table drinking a beer.

"Hey Mama. How have things been with you?"

"Why you keep asking me that Gina?"

"It's been three months and we haven't really talked a lot on the phone. I was just wondering how things have been for you."

"Gina, have we ever just chit-chatted?"

"No ma'am."

"Well, guess what. It ain't about to start now. So just gone about your business and leave me the hell alone."

I got up from the table and walked back to my room. Tears were stinging my eyes as I gently closed the door and lay across the bed. Nothing had changed and I realized that it probably never would. I was here for Lamar and that was what I had to focus on. The next morning I woke up to the smell of bacon. Mmmm, I sure missed the smell of breakfast in the mornings. When I was at school, I would usually end up grabbing an apple or stuffing down a breakfast bar on my way to class. I rarely would go to the cafeteria for breakfast except on Saturday mornings. I had lost weight during my first semester and I really felt good at how slender I had become. Next semester I planned to start going to the gym. I needed to start toning my body and exercising because I was by no means physically fit. My stomach growled, forcing me to roll out from under the warmth of the covers and get dressed. I walked down the hallway enjoying the aroma in the air. Lamar was already at the table.

"Good morning sis. I thought you college students slept until noon every day." he said chuckling.

"Ha ha. Right," I said playfully smacking him on the back of the head, "Good morning Mama."

"Mornin' Gina."

"So Sis, how did it feel to sleep in your old bed again?"

"It felt good, besides, it's not like I have been gone for years Lamar."

"Yeah, but that nice bed in that apartment may have spoiled you."

I laughed at his teasing as Mama set the food on the table and sat down. We blessed the food and ate a hearty breakfast of biscuits, bacon, sausage, eggs, grits, and orange juice. Mama would always cook as if she was feeding a football team and would have to end up saving leftovers for the next day. As we sat there eating Lamar and I chatted about various things while Mama remained silent. Occasionally, she would glance up and look at me or Lamar and then look back down at her plate.

"Mama, Gina and me gonna cook Thanksgiving dinner for you this year."

"What?!" Mama and I exclaimed simultaneously.

"Lamar, you know I don't like nobody in my kitchen."

"Yeah and when did we discuss this?" I asked.

"I know Mama and Gina—girl, stop tripping. I know you can cook. I just thought we'd give Mama a break this year and let her relax while we cooked." Lamar informed me as he sat there munching on a piece of bacon.

"Well, you should have discussed it with me first. It's not that I mind little brother, but it would have been nice to know beforehand. Besides, today is Thanksgiving Eve which means we'll need to start this evening. Right?" I said with an obvious scowl on my face. I can't believe he didn't talk his little plan over with me first before announcing it to Mama.

"Yep. Sorry about springing this on you out of the blue Gina. It just came to me while we were eating breakfast. Well Ma, what you say?"

"Hmmph. Alright, but if y'all mess up my grocery it's gonna be hell to pay." Mama's face didn't match her words because she was smiling at Lamar, but when she turned to look at me, the smile became a look of hatred. I found myself shivering in spite of the warmth from the oven that was still in the kitchen.

"Don't worry we won't." Lamar said as he leaned over and hugged Mama.

She almost choked on her grits and started coughing and sputtering as grits started flying everywhere. "Dammit Lamar. I done told you 'bout that mess. Don't be hugging on me like that."

"Awww Mama. I ain't mean nothing but thank you for letting us do this."

Mama gave him one of her looks as she got up from the table to grab a paper towel and clean herself up. I sat there trying not to smile as I looked at my brother. He had certainly grown up and he was brave. I'd never dare to hug Mama on any occasion. I knew that she wasn't the affectionate type. After breakfast Lamar and I got started on preparing our menu for Thanksgiving. I considered myself a good cook and knew that I wouldn't have a problem with the dinner, but I didn't know about Lamar. I never saw him cook anything before I left home and I wondered if he even knew how to boil water.

"So Lamar, what part of this "dinner" are you going to cook?"

"Sarcasm my dear ain't necessary. I thought I'd do the turkey, dressing, greens, and bread. You can make the pies and cakes. What you think?"

"Oh ok. I got the easy part. You sure you don't want me to help you?"

"Nahh, I got this."

We started cooking around five o'clock. I made pecan pie, sweet potato pie, and a red velvet cake. My prep time was short and I had all of my stuff in the oven baking while Lamar was still working on the turkey. He was mixing different spices together and then began rubbing it on the turkey.

"Boy, are you bathing that bird or seasoning it?"

"Funny. I am puttin' a rub on it. It'll sit in the fridge overnight and then I'm gonna smoke it on the grill tomorrow."

"Huh?"

"Yeah, I saw it on a food network. It's s'posed to come out all juicy and full of flavor."

"Ok." I said skeptically as I watched him apply the seasonings. Once he was done he covered the turkey and put it in the refrigerator. Then he took out the flour, yeast, milk, and sugar.

"What's that for?"

"Yeast rolls."

I started laughing so hard tears rolled down my cheeks. Lamar turned around and he started laughing too.

"Ok, wait a minute. YOU know how to cook yeast rolls?"

"Yeah, Mama showed me."

"Now this I got to see. I can't even make yeast rolls. I can't wait."

"Keep laughing girl. You'll be lickin' your fingers and your plate after you eat my food."

The rest of the evening flew by as I watched my little brother cook. He made an oyster stuffing for the turkey instead of Mama's usual cornbread dressing. He put the yeast dough in the refrigerator overnight and said that he would bake the rolls right before we ate on Thanksgiving day. The kitchen was warm from the oven and it smelled of pies, cakes, and seasoning as we sat there and talked. Mama walked by a couple of times from the living room to the bedroom. I could hear the TV on and knew that she was probably watching one of her favorite shows. I was surprised that she hadn't come into kitchen at least once, but she didn't. After Lamar and I finished we cleaned up the kitchen and went into the living room to watch TV with Mama. She had found some movie on and we sat there and watched it with her. I looked over into the corner at the Christmas tree that Mama had already put up before I got home. It was an artificial tree that was about five feet tall. The white lights twinkled from amidst the green branches as silver and gold ornaments sparkled from the light. There were no presents under the tree which was no surprise. Mama probably had some stuff on lay-away for Lamar and wouldn't get it out until the first of December. We sat up late that night and ended up with Mama telling old stories about our grandparents. She was in a jolly mood and was laughing as she reminisced. Now I understood the trips back and forth to the bedroom. She must have had a bottle of her favorite gin in there and had been sipping on that while Lamar and I cooked. Lamar and I sat up and talked past midnight after we finished cooking before I finally called it a night.

I skipped breakfast the next morning to save room for dinner. Thanksgiving Day turned out to be quite enjoyable. The food was delicious and even Mama said so. Lamar's rolls practically melted in my mouth and I had popped about three of them before I realized it. The turkey was the best that I've ever had and I ended up eating two helpings of it. I used my roll to sop up the last bit of gravy from my plate.

"See, I told you. You may not be lickin' the plate, but you sho' sopping it." he said laughing.

"Oh be quiet. Lamar, I didn't know you could cook like this. When did you learn how to cook like this?"

"Well, I been experimenting since you left. Mama been letting me cook almost every day."

"Yeah, my baby gifted. See Gina you ain't the only one in this house who got talent."

"Lamar, I'm impressed. Everything was great! You got skills!"

"Thanks, sis. I think I know what I want to do after high school."

"What?"

"Go to cooking...I mean culinary school."

"Really?" I asked in surprise.

"Yeah, you think that'll be a good thing to do?"

"Lamar, it's about doing what makes you happy. If you enjoy cooking and have a passion for it, then I think you should do it."

"Thanks. Now, my next question, is there a school near you that offers that?"

"Actually, there is a school right outside of Boxley that offers that degree. It's about thirty miles away in Lansdale. You know, I could get you some information when I go back."

"Cool. "

"Lamar, you still got three mo' years to make up yo' mind." Mama interjected.

"But Ma I know this is what I want to do. I want to learn as much as I can about it now.'

"Hmmph. You gonna leave me too Lamar. What I'm gonna do here by myself? Who gonna help me...?"

"Ma, don't go getting yourself all upset. Let's change the subject."

"Gina, you been fillin' his head with this mess. Since you been in this world, all you done is take everythang from me. You ain't been nothin' but a burden since the day you was born. I ain't letting you take my son, you hear me!." Mama yelled as she threw her glass of tea into my face.

"Ma, c'mon. Why you do that?" Lamar asked.

"Watch yo' self Lamar. I can still whip your ass."

Mama came and stood over me breathing hard. I looked up at her with tears in my eyes trying to figure out why she hated me so much.

"Gina, this is yo' last time in my house. I don't want you here no mo'. You find you somewhere else to go for Christmas."

"Why Mama? Why don't you love me?" I asked as the tears flowed down. I didn't care what she did to me. I needed answers for all the years of suffering from her abuse.

"I don't have to explain nothing to you, but I'm gonna tell you why you make me sick every time I look at you." Mama leaned over so close to me that I could feel her breath on my cheek. Her lips were pulled back over her teeth in a thin line as she spoke. "Every time I see you and look into yo' face you remind me of the man who raped me. I thought I could raise you like my normal child and love you Gina, but I couldn't. I hated your daddy and I hated you all these years. I should have aborted you like I started to, but your grandma wouldn't let me! You've been a constant reminder of the worst day of my life all these years! "

"What?!" I cried. I felt sick. A wave of nausea rushed over me and I could feel the warm salty saliva building up in my mouth. There was a rushing noise in my ears.

"Yeah Miss High and Mighty. Yo' daddy raped me! I was attacked one night coming home from a friend's house and ended up pregnant with you. My folks didn't believe in abortion or giving up a child. So, I had no choice but to raise you myself."

Mama's face was twisted with anger as she said those words to me. As I sat there I felt that the room was spinning out of control. Everything went dark as I fainted.

"Gina, Gina.?"

I moaned as I slowly opened my eyes to see Lamar sitting beside my bed. I could feel a cool towel on my forehead and realized that he must have put it there.

"Lamar, did I faint?" I whispered.

"Yep. You fell right out of the chair. I checked to make sure you didn't hit your head. I couldn't feel any bumps or anything. You feel okay?"

"You kidding me? No, I'm not ok. Lamar, I can't believe what Mama said. All these years I thought you and me had the same daddy, but we don't. How can Mama hate me so? I'm still a part of her."

"Gina, I don't know. I'm so sorry."

Lamar started crying and I did too. I was touched by the compassion my brother had for me. I never thought we would have grown to be so close and have such a good relationship. We cried and talked for most of the night. I asked him to help me find a ride to the bus station the next day so I could leave. I told Lamar that I loved him with all of my heart and that we would continue to talk as often as possible on the phone. I told him that I'd never be coming back to Pikesville again and he would be welcome to come and visit me at anytime. The next day I packed my bags and left Mama's house for the last time.

Chapter 15
A Past Acquaintance

The semester after Thanksgiving passed by uneventfully and I barely passed my courses. I sank into a state of depression and spent the first two weeks of the semester sleeping. My roommate Celeste had noticed my behavior and had tried to talk to me. I told her that I was fine and not to worry. After awhile she left me to drown in my sorrows. My other two roommates and I were cordial, but never developed any type of relationship so they didn't make any comments one way or the other. The summer was drawing near and I needed to find a job so that I could stay on campus and take some summer courses. I had no idea what kind of job I could find that was close enough to the school so that I wouldn't have to worry about transportation for getting to work. It was the week of final exams and I had just finished taking my psychology exam and was walking across campus to the café for a snack.

"Hey!"

Someone was yelling from behind me and since there was no one in front of me I figured he was talking to me. I turned around to see if I had dropped something.

"Hey, can I walk with you?"

The sun was shining in my face and I put my hands above my eyes to block out some of the light. I saw a guy running to catch up and when he got closer I looked up into a pair of warm brown eyes. He must have been about six feet four inches which was just a little shorter than my brother Lamar. His skin was the color of milk chocolate and there was something very familiar about him.

"Excuse me?"

"You don't remember me do you?"

"Did we take a class together or something?"

"No. You really don't remember do you? My name is Sebastian Mallard."

I looked at him again. Oh my goodness! It was the boy from the summer that I went to the store for Mama and ended up in the hospital because I was ten minutes late.

"It can't be." I said incredulously.

"Yeah, small world I know." He said smiling down at me. Had I ever seen teeth that white or even on anyone I thought to myself?

"Hello?" Not only was he smiling now, but his eyes were twinkling as if he was reading my thoughts. Get a grip girl I told myself.

"How did you know it was me?" I finally asked with a frown, hoping that it would wipe that smile off of his face.

"The memory of how you looked and your shape is engraved in my mind."

"Don't be fresh." I snapped back with the coldest stare that I could muster.

"Sorry, I am not trying to disrespect you or anything. It seems like I have a habit of starting out on the wrong foot with you. What I meant was that you have an athletic looking body. You're taller than most girls I know."

"Uh-huh. That's original." In spite of myself I smiled.

"May I walk with you?"

I hesitated, "Look, I really am not interested in…"

"Stop, don't finish that. All I want to do is walk with you. I don't know, maybe even be your friend. Something tells me that you need a friend."

Was he trying to play me? I looked at him again and saw nothing on his face but sincerity. I usually was good at reading people and followed my instincts about them. Sebastian didn't seem to pose a threat and something told me that he might be a pretty cool guy.

"Ok. I'm on my way to the café to grab a snack before my next final. You're welcome to come."

"Thanks. What's your name again?"

"Oh, you didn't remember that huh?"

He smiled showing those pearly white teeth. "No, I forgot your name."

"It's Gina."

"Gina, that's right. Cool, let's go to the café."

Sebastian and I ended up talking for over thirty minutes in which he did most of the talking. I found out that he had been visiting his cousins in Pikesville for the summer that first time we met. His father was the pastor of a local church in Boxley, Trinity Baptist Church, which was less than a mile away from the campus.

"So, are you going home for the summer?"

"Uh no. I am going to take some summer courses and stay here. I need to find a job for the summer."

"Really? There is a job opening at my dad's church. They are looking for an office receptionist. Ms. Jenkins, our full-time receptionist, just had a baby and asked for a two month leave. Why don't you apply?"

"I don't know."

"It pays well. I promise you won't find anything else that pays as much."

I thought about it and realized that this could actually be a blessing. I really needed to make some good money this summer. I told him that I would apply and come down to the church after my last final was over on Wednesday.

"Good, if you come later in the afternoon you could stay for our bible study."

"I don't know about that."

"Well, think about it. Our church is not huge, but it is not small either."

"Ok. I'll think about it and thanks again for the information about the job."

"No problem." he said as he glanced at his watch. "Gotta run Gina. We both have a final in about fifteen minutes. Hopefully, I'll see you again soon."

"Nice talking to you." I said as he walked away. He sure seemed like a nice guy and he was handsome too. His faded blue jeans looked freshly pressed and fit his frame in a baggy fashion. He was wearing a dark blue and white striped button up shirt and black casual Rockports. Even in his casual outfit something about him stood out from the rest of the guys I had seen around campus. I thought about how odd it was that I ended up at Boxley which was the very town where he lived. I had been on campus a whole year and had not met him until this very moment when I needed a job. I knew that it could only be God working in my life for such an opportunity to come by.

My last few months had been very difficult emotionally. The night that Mama told me everything about my biological father, left me in a state of shock. I felt like a zombie walking around campus the first couple of months afterwards. Inwardly, there was nothing left and I didn't even care. I had no desire for relationships, not even friendships.

However, talking to Sebastian had seemed comforting somehow. I packed up my belongings, swung my backpack over my shoulder, and headed to take my next final.

Wednesday afternoon was a beautiful clear, sunny day and perfect for walking the short distance to Trinity Baptist. I couldn't remember seeing the church when I drove around town when first coming to Boxley. I rounded the corner of the last block and saw the church just ahead. It was huge! Didn't Sebastian say that it was kind of medium-sized I asked myself as I continued walking? That boy needed to take some math and learn a few things about estimating sizes and stuff. The church stood on the corner of Moreland and Trace Ave. It was white on all sides and had a large steeple on top of it. The landscape was just as beautiful as the building with its green plush lawn and perfectly trimmed hedges that lined both sides of the walkway leading to the front door. The front door was really two doors with oval shaped stained glass windows decorating each of them.

I walked up to the building and found the front door to be unlocked. I stood in the foyer admiring the hardwood floors and the beautiful glass chandelier that hung down from the ceiling. To my right was a long hallway with its shiny hardwood floor and on the wall was a sign indicating the office numbers of each employee. Sebastian had told me that I needed to get an application from the secretary and fill it out while I waited to see his father for a brief interview. I walked down the long hallway into a large open area where the offices were located. I looked to the left and saw the secretary's office. I knocked on the door and was told to come in.

"Hi, my name is Gina Jones. I'm here to apply for a job."

"Come on in dear. Yes, I've been expecting you. My name is Joyce Allen, the church secretary, and around here everybody calls me Miss Joyce. Have a seat."

I sat down in the chair opposite of her desk and waited as she shuffled through some papers. Ms. Allen was a middle-aged woman with black hair that was just showing the early signs of graying at the temple. She was wearing a business style dark blue skirt and jacket with matching shoes. The smile that she had shown when I walked through the door had been genuine. I liked her immediately.

"Ok dear, here is the application. You can go ahead and fill that out right here and then I will show you to Pastor Mallard's office for the interview."

It took me about five minutes or so to complete the application before I handed it back to Ms. Allen. She looked it over and told me that everything was filled out correctly and led me out of the office down the hallway to the pastor's door. She asked me to wait in the hallway for a moment as she walked into the office.

I heard her say, "Pastor Mallard, the young lady is here to interview for the receptionist position," just as the door closed behind her. In less than a minute the door opened again and she motioned for me to come in.

"Pastor, this young lady is Gina Jones. Gina, this is Pastor Mallard." Miss Joyce said as she introduced us to each other.

"Ah yes, please come in." he said. His voice had a deep, rich sound as he spoke.

I followed her through the door and saw Pastor Mallard sitting behind his cherry wood desk. He was wearing a charcoal gray, pin-striped suit. He stood up as we came into the office and I was amazed at his height. He was just as tall as his son. He had the same milk chocolate complexion and piercing brown eyes. He smiled came forward and extended his hand to me. I extended my hand and gave him a brief, but firm handshake.

"Well, Ms. Allen, I think I can take it from here. Thank you. Gina, please have a seat." he motioned to a chair directly in front of his desk. He had walked back around his desk and sat back down.

"You're welcome Pastor. Gina, I hope to be seeing more of you," she said as she walked out of the office and closed the door.

"Gina, I've heard some good things about you from my son, Sebastian. He told me of how you two met a few years ago."

"Really?"

Pastor Mallard smiled as he looked at the surprised look on my face. "Yes, my son and I talk about most things that happen in his life. He's a good kid. So, let's start with the interview shall we?"

Pastor Mallard interviewed me for twenty five minutes as he asked general questions about school and what did I want to do once I graduated. He asked me about my faith and if I had found a church to attend while I was at school in Boxley. He inquired of my secretarial skills and he wanted to know if I had any type of phone etiquette. We even went through different phone conversation scenarios to see how well I communicated with people on the phone. By the end of the interview he said that he was very impressed with me. He thought I had the right attitude and personality for the job.

"Gina, can you start next Monday?"

"Next Monday?" I asked surprisedly.

"Yes, will that be a problem for you?"

"N-n-no sir. Monday will work well."

"Good, the job is yours if you want it."

"Oh thank you so much Pastor Mallard. Thank you." I felt myself getting teary eyed and had to take a deep breath to control the tears.

"You're welcome. Just go and talk to Ms. Allen and she will give you a job description and have you fill out the paperwork needed for paying you each month. If you have any questions, then Ms. Allen will be able to help you or you can feel free to come see me."

"Thank you again sir." I said as I stood and left the office to head back to Ms. Allen's office. I was so happy I could have turned a cartwheel right there. I had a job! It was a good one too with great pay! It was around five o'clock by the time I had finished going over everything with the secretary.

"Gina dear, since it's so close to time for our fellowship dinner to start, why don't you join us this evening for dinner and bible study?" Miss Joyce said as I was standing up to leave.

"Well, I don't really know anyone and…"

"Oh don't worry about that, we have some very friendly and caring members here. You'll soon get to know most of them. Besides you know me and you can hang out with me." She said with a gentle smile.

I had no choice but to accept the invitation. I sat in Miss Joyce's office until she finished up her work. She chatted with me as she was typing some last minute letters that the pastor needed by the end of the day. I learned that Miss Joyce was fifty and a widower. She didn't have any kids, but she had a love for young people and usually took most of the college students who attended Trinity under her wing. She told me that she often had students over for dinner on Sundays after church. As I sat listening to her, I felt such a peaceful feeling come over me sitting there in her office. I wondered why she didn't have any kids because she would have been a great mother. I thought of Mama and tears started stinging my eyes.

"Honey, what's wrong?"

"Ma'am?" I didn't realize Miss Joyce had been asking me something.

"I had asked about your family. I turned around and saw you looking all teary eyed. Is there something wrong?" I could see the concern on her face and that made the tears even harder to keep back.

"No ma'am. My allergies bother me sometimes."

"Oh ok. Listen Gina, I know you don't know me from a man in the moon, but if you ever need someone to talk to then I am here. From the moment you walked in that door I knew in my spirit that the Lord had sent you here for a specific reason and it has nothing to do with the job that you got today."

Under different circumstances, I would have thought that she was either losing her mind or pretending to care when she really different. I knew that everything she was saying was true. Although I had thought about not applying for the job, I wasn't so full of pride that I had not recognized that meeting Sebastian again and finding out about this job was more than a mere coincidence. The depression that had overcome me the past year was worst than anything I had felt before. I was tired of living my life isolated and feeling rejected and unloved. I wanted to experience the fullness of joy that God had for me, but I needed to resolve all of the issues that weighing me down. I had been praying for God to show me how to get past all of the hurt and anger.

"Miss Joyce, I know that God sent me here too. I have been praying for answers about some things, but I'm just not ready to talk about it. You are one of the first people that I've ever felt really comfortable with after meeting the first time. Thank you for being so nice to me."

Miss Joyce asked if I minded her hugging me and I shocked myself by saying that it was okay. She came from behind her desk and embraced me as if I was her own. I couldn't help myself, the flood gates opened and the tears poured down for all the years that I longed for a mother's love and nurturing. I cried for the child in me that had been deprived of essential human needs.

Chapter 16
New Experiences

Over the next month I sank into a routine as office receptionist. I answered the phone, handled the mail, and assigned appointments for Pastor Mallard. My desk was out front in the foyer area near the front door of the church. I enjoyed meeting and greeting people because it was helping me to come out of my shell. Everyone commented on how cordial I was and Miss Joyce and Pastor Mallard told me how happy they were that God sent me to them. I had been attending bible study and church services since my job started and had thoroughly enjoyed the teachings of Pastor Mallard. Every Sunday he would open up the doors of the church and invite the unsaved or the saved that needed a church home. Each time I remained in my seat and waited for him to move on. I just didn't feel ready to become a member yet. I saw Sebastian almost every day because he made it a point to stop by my desk and chat. We had even hung out a couple of times and gone to the skating rink or to the movies. He was definitely not like all of the other boys. He never tried to make a pass at me and was always respectful. As I sat thinking about him, I realized that he and I were becoming good friends. I could talk to him easily and he would listen and at times had some good advice to give.

It was Friday evening and I was packing up my things and straightening my desk as I got ready to leave for the day when Sebastian came in.

"Hey Gina. You almost done?"

"Hi, yes. I was just packing my things. What's up?" I asked without looking up and continued to gather my things.

"My parents and I are going to hang out tonight and go out to dinner and then see that new Denzel movie. You want to come?"

"Well," I hesitated before answering, "with your parents?"

"Yes. They don't bite you know." he said smiling. "Besides both of them think that you are quite special and they know that we have become good friends. So what do you say?"

"Ok."

"Good. We'll pick you up around six thirty at your apartment." he said as he started down the hall towards his dad's office.

What had I just done to myself by agreeing to hang out with the Mallards? I had only talked to Mrs. Mallard on occasion in passing. Every time I talked to Pastor Mallard it was work associated. I wondered if I could come up with an excuse and tell Sebastian that I wouldn't be able to make it. Nahh, I told myself that would be rude. Oh well, maybe it wouldn't be as bad as I thought.

I left the church and hurried to the apartment to choose something to wear. I had about an hour before the Mallards would be coming by. I chose a pair of cuffed, cream colored slacks and brown shell top to wear. I didn't want to be too dressy, but not too casual either so I slipped on a pair of brown strapless, sandals with a one inch heel. I pulled my hair back into a ponytail and held it in place with a brown hair clip. I looked myself over in the mirror in my bedroom and realized I looked quite good, but just to enhance the naturalness, I added a touch of eye shadow and some lip gloss. I had gotten my hair relaxed for the first time two weeks ago and the beautician had trimmed the ends. I was shocked at how much my hair had grown, it was on my shoulders. I came down the stairs to wait for Sebastian and his parents. Celeste was sitting on the sofa watching a movie. She and I were the only two in the apartment for the summer.

"Oooohhh, Gina. Girl you look sharp. Let me guess, a hot date with Sebastian?" she asked rolling her eyes and fanning herself dramatically.

I laughed, "Celeste, girl I've told you that you should be on stage somewhere with all that drama. And nooo, it's not a hot date. I am hanging out with Sebastian and his parents tonight."

"Oh, the parents? Now that sounds kind of serious."

"Nahh, he and I are good friends and that's it. He's never tried anything with me."

"He's just waiting to make his move girl."

"He knows where I stand and he accepts it. Now stop teasing me."

"Ok, ok. You do look good Gina. You're very pretty."

"Now you making me blush. You have any plans for tonight?"

"Yep, sitting right here eating popcorn and watching movies. You know that's my favorite thing to do on Fridays."

"Well, enjoy yourself and I'll hang with you when I come back." I said as the doorbell rang.

"Enjoy yourself Gina."

I opened the door and took a step back when I saw Sebastian standing there. He was wearing a pair of cream-colored slacks and a brown button up shirt. He looked at me and started grinning.

"Are you a peeping Tom, Sebastian?" I asked teasingly.

"No. I can't believe we are wearing the same thing. Now that is a coincidence. Come on, my parents are in the car."

We walked to the parking lot and Sebastian opened my door as we got into Pastor Mallard's black Infinity.

"Good evening Gina dear. Did you two plan to dress alike? Mrs. Mallard asked me smiling.

I blushed. "No ma'am. It's a pure coincidence," I said as I settled into my seat and put my seatbelt on.

Pastor Mallard chuckled and looked at his wife. They both smiled at each other exchanging a look that went beyond my understanding. We ended up eating one of the upscale Italian restaurants. I sat looking at the Mallard family as they talked back and forth to each other. Three months ago I never would have thought that my life could have changed so quickly. I was more outgoing than I'd ever been and I was beginning to feel comfortable around new people. Sitting here tonight I was actually experiencing how a real family interacted with each other. I looked at Mrs. Mallard and admired her beauty. She was about two shades lighter than her husband. She had long black hair that was normally worn in curls. Mrs. Mallard was slender and I learned that she worked out in the local gym about four times a week to stay that way. She was active in the church working with the women and the children.

"Gina, Sebastian tells us that you are from the same town as my younger brother." Mrs. Mallard said.

"Yes ma'am. I am."

"Do you have brothers or sisters?"

I told her that I had a younger brother who I kept in touch with on a regular basis and that he had plans to attend the culinary school near Boxley. She asked me about my mom and my dad. "Uhh, my mom raised me by herself." I said

"Meredith dear. Don't start prying now." Pastor Mallard's voice was soft and cajoling as he patted his wife on the arm.

"I'm not Herb. I was just trying to learn a little bit more about Gina. I'm sorry dear if it seemed I was prying. Would you rather not talk about it?"

It was strange to hear Pastor Mallard called by his first name, Herbert. His full name was Herbert William Mallard III. "Well, I never really knew my dad."

"That must have been hard for you," said Mrs. Mallard with compassion on her face.

"Yes it was." I managed to say with a smile to let them know that I was fine with talking about it.

Sebastian interjected and we started talking about school. The rest of dinner was uneventful and we left the restaurant and went to the movie theater. I ended up sitting between Sebastian and his mom who sat next to Pastor Mallard. After the movie was over we ended up going out for ice cream. By the time I got back to the apartment I was exhausted, but happy for having one of the most enjoyable evenings in my life. Celeste was sound asleep on the sofa and the television was still on. I turned it off and picked up the blanket off of the floor and covered her up.

Chapter 17
The Breakthrough

On Saturday I lounged around the apartment in my pajamas until late afternoon. Celeste and I went to the dining hall for dinner and went back to the apartment to watch movies. Before going to bed I picked out my clothes for church the next morning. I decided to wear a turquoise skirt with scalloped designs and a matching top. The next morning I got up, dressed and flat ironed my hair. I'd decided to wear it down today which was something I rarely did because it was so thick and that made my neck hot during the summer. I'd been trying to get Celeste to come to church with me, but each time she always came up with an excuse. I walked the short distance to the church and went to sit down in my usual spot in the middle section. Praise and worship was high and the spirit was flowing this morning. I even found myself standing up clapping and praising. Pastor Mallard finally came up to give his sermon.

"This morning church, we will be reading from the book of Genesis chapter fifty and verse twenty. Please stand for the reading of God's word." The whole congregation stood up as he read the passage of scripture.

"My title this morning is: 'They Tried to Kill You; But God Stepped In." You may be seated in his presence."

My skin began to tingle as I sat down and re-read the scripture that Pastor Mallard was preaching from. I took out my pen and paper to take notes as he started. He summarized the events leading up to the particular verse by telling us of how Joseph's brother was jealous of him because he was favored by his father. They made plans to kill him, but instead decided to sell him into slavery. He went on to talk about the famine that caused the brothers to travel to Egypt for food which eventually led to their re-acquaintance with Joseph. In chapter fifty he told us how Jacob had died and now the brothers wanted his forgiveness and were afraid of him, but Joseph told them not to be afraid because what they had meant for harm; God meant it for good for such a time as this had come.

"There are people in this sanctuary this morning that have gone through some trials and tribulations in your lives that were meant to harm you, but God has turned it around for your good. However, you still haven't come to recognize his goodness. You're still wounded and hurt by those things that happened to you. You can't fully live the life that God has ordained for you because you still hurting. God says it's time for you to forgive those who hurt you and allow him to heal you."

There were shouts of hallelujah and amen as the congregation clapped and praised God. Pastor Mallard continued. "Aren't you tired of being angry? Tired of feeling bound while the very people who hurt you are living their lives as if nothing happened? Healing is here today. The presence of the Lord is here and he desires to heal your wounds today. For those who have a desire to be healed, come to the altar."

Something wet was hitting my hands and I realized it was my own tears. As I sat there listening once again the flood gates opened like they did that day in Miss Joyce's office. I felt myself standing up and walking down the aisle towards the altar. The closer I got the more the tears poured down. I heard someone crying and realized that it was me. I couldn't stop the tears and my whole body began to shake. I felt a pair of gentle arms encircle me and without looking I knew that it was Miss Joyce. She said nothing but just held me as I leaned on her shoulders and cried. Pastor Mallard came down and laid hands on me and prayed that I allow God to heal every area that was hurting. He thanked God for my breakthrough and prayed that from this point forward that I would begin to experience the fullness of his joy and love. I could feel the Holy Spirit inside of me and a shout arose from my belly that my mouth could not contain. I began to dance and praise God as the shout turned into words of thanksgiving and giving God the glory. The more I danced and the more I praised God; the more I could feel the chains falling off. It was time for my healing and I was ready. I wanted to discover the person that God had created me to be. I ended up becoming a member of Trinity Baptist that day.

After church Miss Joyce invited me over to her house for dinner and I accepted. It took us about twenty minutes to get to her house from the church. As she turned into her neighborhood I admired the traditional style homes with their well manicured lawns. There were brick homes, wood siding ones. and some were even stucco. Miss Joyce turned into her driveway leading up to a two story brick home surrounded by shade trees. Her front yard was beautifully decorated with blooming flowers of red and pink. She pulled around to the back door and we got out and entered through the kitchen. Miss Joyce had good taste and her house was decorated in style. She had hardwood floors throughout the house and each room had a color scheme. Her kitchen consisted of oak cabinets and matching table and chairs with marble countertops. The pale yellow paint made it seem sunny and cheerful.

"Have a seat at the table Gina dear while I heat up the food."

"You sure you don't want me to help Miss Joyce."

"No, it's not any trouble at all. We can chat while I get things ready. You'll be my only guest today because I figured it was time we talked."

"Yes ma'am. I kind of figured as much and I agree. You mind if I start while you are warming everything up?"

"Of course not, whatever makes you feel comfortable."

I started with my earliest memories of when things with Mama turned for the worst and I gave Miss Joyce a detailed account of the years of emotional and physical abuse that I had suffered. I told her the things I had learned about my biological father last Thanksgiving and the things Mama had said to me. By the time I had finished my story Miss Joyce was in tears. She came over and hugged me and then sat down. She prayed with me before she began to talk. Miss Joyce told me how much she admired my strength and courage to keep moving forward in spite of my situations. She also thought it would be a good idea to seek counseling and recommended Pastor Mallard since I knew him and would probably be more comfortable with him. I told her that I would start scheduling counseling sessions with him as soon as he was available because I was eager to begin resolving my past issues.

Over the next six months my life changed drastically. I met with Pastor Mallard for counseling twice each week. I learned to let go of the anger that I felt towards Mama, Mr. Carl, and my biological father. I also learned to let go of the guilt I felt for not being stronger and telling someone about the rape. I forgave each person who had hurt me and I began to pray for their deliverance. Miss Joyce and I spent a lot of time together on the weekends and she told me that she considered me to be like a daughter to her. You would have thought she was my mother the way she nurtured me and fussed over me. I grew to love her like a mother. Lamar and I still talked almost every day and I was proud of how much he had matured. We ended up spending the following Christmas together at Miss Joyce's house. She fell in love with Lamar and started calling him her son.

Sebastian and I are the very best of friends and I was finally able to tell him my entire life story. He and I cried together at the end and he held me for the longest time. Instead of the repulsion I usually felt when near a male, it was the opposite. I felt safe and protected. I don't know what the future holds for Sebastian and me, but I am thankful that he is my best friend. I thank God for his grace and mercy that brought me through the difficult times in my life. Even more so, I am thankful for the people that he placed in my life who have given me the human love and nurturing that I missed out on as a child.

Pastor Mallard found a way to keep me employed after the

summer months were over by appointing me as youth director of a mentoring program for teen girls. He told me that I could work on it part-time during the school months and hopefully by the following summer it would be ready to operate. I look forward to helping young girls who may have gone through or are in the midst of similar situations that I had to endure. To God be the Glory!